Desires of Christmas Present
A Christmas Carol
Book 2

Desires of Christmas Present
A Christmas Carol
Book 2

BY

LEXI POST

Desires of Christmas Present:

A Christmas Carol, Book 2 Summary

Kentucky born and bred, Coco Baker, has just been given the assignment of her spirit guide career, but she's forced to partner with a Scottish upper class snob who thinks he knows what's best for their living client. Despite him, she's determined to do well on this case and find out what the arrogant man is hiding. Unfortunately, she discovers that sometimes not knowing is better…for everyone.

Acknowledgments

For Bob Fabich, Sr., my very own Christmas present. And for my sister Paige Wood, who understands why this book was born.

Thank you to my daughter-in-law Rebecca Curran Fabich (and her parents) who let me ask a zillion questions regarding daily life in Scotland today.

As usual, my critique partner, Marie Patrick, was critical in getting this story whipped into shape and out on time.

And I can't close without thanking my fantastic readers who leave reviews that inspire me to write more and more. You all are awesome!

Author's Note

Desires of Christmas Present was inspired by *A Christmas Carol* by Charles Dickens. In Dickens' story, Ebenezer Scrooge, a miserly curmudgeon, is told by the spirit of his former business partner, Marley, that he will be visited by three ghosts and if he doesn't change his ways he will pay for it in the afterlife. Scrooge scoffs at the idea but as he journeys into his past, present, and future with the spirit of each period of his life, he sees the error of his ways and becomes a completely different man when he wakes up on Christmas day.

But what if the spirit itself, as well as the living human, was in need of help, and the visit could make a difference in the existence of both? Could the Spirits of Christmas Present come to terms with their former lives while helping a young woman rejoin her own? What secrets might be revealed about her, themselves and their superior, the woman's late husband? And most importantly, can love conquer all even in the afterlife?

Chapter One

Arrogant. Asshole.

Those were the only two words that came to mind when Coco Baker heard the name, Ian Fergusson. Taken separately or together, they described him to a tee. "I'm sorry, but there's no way I can work with Ian Fergusson." She gripped the back of the chair in front of her. The man pissed her off simply by existing.

She didn't know how he'd ever been chosen as a spirit guide. She couldn't believe that the Scottish snob had ever had to work a day in his life. From what she'd seen, he didn't get along with any of the other spirit guides…or other spirits for that matter. Telling live people how they should feel and act just didn't work, and she was positive that's how he did his job.

Cameron Douglas, her boss, shook his head, his sandy brown hair falling onto his forehead with the movement. "I need two of you on this case. It's too hard a task for just one."

Oh, that was fine. "I can work with someone else, or if you like, I can bow out and wait for the next case." She'd just have to make it up to whoever was unlucky enough to be assigned to work with Ian.

Cameron leaned forward, setting his large arms on his desk and clasping his hands in front of him. "I'm afraid I need you, in particular, on this case."

"Me?" Had he noticed her track record? She'd begun to think only the spirits who knew spirits ever got promoted.

"Yes, you. I need your special instinct."

She flushed. "You know about that?"

"I do. It's nothing to be ashamed of, and on this assignment it will be very important."

She dropped into the chair in front of her boss's desk. When she became a spirit, she was surprised to discover her ability to recognize soulmates was still with her, but only among the living. It had helped her succeed on more than one case, but it felt as if she cheated when she used it. "Does this assignment have to do with helping someone find their true love?"

"No. I'll explain as soon as Ian arrives."

Despite her dislike of the man, she looked forward to seeing him. It was a pity he was such an ass because his body was to die for. Not that she'd seen him in anything but nice clothes. Casual for that man was a polo shirt and slacks, but his broad shoulders, narrow waist and rounded ass filled it all out quite nicely.

She preferred casual, especially the flutter shirt she wore. The pink stripes went with the streak in her hair and the three-quarter, wide sleeves hid what she considered her large upper arms.

Cameron shifted in his seat, obviously growing impatient.

She didn't like uncomfortable silences, especially with her boss. "Since we're waiting, could you tell me if Mrs. Maxwell is doing any better? I know I helped her see that she could still celebrate Christmas even though she was in a wheelchair, but I didn't run into Joy since she got back. Did all go as planned?"

Cameron relaxed, his smile quick. "Mrs. Maxwell is doing very well. The three of you did an excellent job with her."

She'd really liked the old widow and could see that her true soulmate had passed away. It hadn't been easy finding the right people to visit so Mrs. Maxwell could see she still had a purpose in life and a reason to live. "I'm glad. That woman has so much love to give, it would be a pity for it to end too soon. I think mankind needs as many people like her as it can get."

"I agree." Cameron sighed. "Unfortunately, Christmas can be the time of year when those very people find it the most difficult to keep going."

Boy, he could say that again. She'd seen far too many cases like Mrs. Maxwell's since she'd become a spirit guide.

Ian held Lucy's tiny hand firmly as he flew them over the rooftops of Glasgow, her silence an oddity after all her chattering this night. When they landed back in her bedroom, he let go and knelt in front of her. "Do you understand now?"

The eight-year-old nodded. "I do. Thank you for showing me. I promise I will be strong and not let anyone bully me into thinking I'm worthless." She pressed her finger against her chest. "I'm worth a million pounds!"

He smiled. "That's right. And what about the bullies?"

Her wide smile dimmed. "I feel sorry for them. I didn't know."

"Come here." He opened his arms wide and Lucy stepped into them. Hugging her was a balm for his soul that wouldn't last, but he craved it nonetheless.

Her pudgy little arms finally released him, and there was a tear in her eye.

"Now, Pumpkin. No weeping. Remember you still have another visitor coming tonight."

Her face brightened immediately. "Will he be as braw as you?"

Ian chuckled. "I don't know. It could very well be a woman who can talk dresses and dolls with you."

"I want a braw man." She crossed her arms over her chest and frowned at him.

He lowered his brow. "Now Lucy, remember what I said about

how special you are. You don't want me to cancel the next spirit altogether, do you?"

Her eyes widened. "Oh, no." She grabbed his arm. "Please let the spirit come."

He kissed her on the tip of her nose before rising to his full height. "All right, Pumpkin. I'll send the next spirit. Now let's return you to normal."

She stood still with her arms wide. "I'm ready."

He placed his hand on her shoulder and unphased her, his physical connection with her at an end. "Now you crawl into bed and take a nap." He glanced at the clock. "Your next visitor will be here in an hour and you want to be fresh for your trip into the future."

She smiled and ran to her small bed. Scrambling into it, she pulled the covers up to her chin. "Can you kiss me goodbye?"

His heart swelled. "Of course." If it wasn't for his assignments, he probably would have faded into nothingness, like he'd heard some spirits had done.

Brushing Lucy's cheek with his hand, though she couldn't feel it, he bent and kissed her there.

"And this one." She turned her head and pointed to her other cheek.

He obediently kissed the other one.

"And here." She pointed to her nose and he chuckled.

"Okay, last one." He kissed her button nose. "Happy dreams."

She nodded and waved. "Bye."

He floated toward her ceiling and waved back.

Once above the roof, he headed for his supervisor's office, the warmth and peace of Lucy leaving him the faster he flew. A tiny flicker of hope remained, his craving for another case already urging him on.

With no time in the afterlife, he was outside Cameron's door in a moment. Opening it, he stepped inside.

~~*~~

Coco turned around in her chair. Ian Fergusson stood just inside the door. His tall, broad-shouldered physique looked hard beneath his golf shirt even while relaxed. His face was equally hard as were his steel grey eyes. His angular jaw and sharp nose with a slight hook downward would have been enough to warn anyone to stay away, and beneath his short red hair were equally sharp ears. Everything about him was unrelenting.

He looked down his nose at her before raising his gaze to Cameron who had stood at his entrance. "I was informed that you needed me for a case. I can come back when you're done."

Her boss held out his hand and smiled. "No, come in. You'll be working with Coco on this one."

Ian raised an eyebrow and strode forward to clasp Cameron's hand. "I was unaware you ever sent two spirit guides on one case. I have always worked alone. I complete my assignment successfully that way."

Cameron nodded as he sat again. "Please." He motioned toward the other chair.

"I'm good." Ian waved him off.

Coco gritted her teeth. That was so like him. He thought he was above them all and could do what he wanted. She turned her gaze to Cameron. "Why do you need two of us?"

Ian frowned. "Yes. I can't imagine a case so difficult that it takes two spirit guides."

A team player he was not, but she'd already known that.

Cameron studied her, then Ian. When his gaze drifted between them, it was obvious that whatever he was about to say was important. Finally, he spoke, but didn't make eye contact with either of them. "Your case is my wife."

Shocked, she sat forward in her chair. "Your wife? But I thought—"

Ian interrupted her. "I was of the understanding that we were not allowed to take assignments directly related to us."

Cameron's gaze moved to Ian. "We aren't. However, this case has been given approval by Remiel."

"I didn't realize special dispensation was possible."

Seriously? She swallowed an exasperated sigh. "That's exactly what Cameron just said." Dimwit. She shook her head at Ian.

He didn't even acknowledge her, his gaze riveted to Cameron.

Her boss stared Ian down, which gave her a certain amount of satisfaction. Cameron's voice was hard. "This is a unique circumstance, Ian."

Her new "partner" had the grace to back down. Shoot, how was she going to control him if he tried pulling that crap on her? Maybe she needed to channel Cameron's deep tones.

The silence grew awkward so she jumped in. "What can we do for your wife?"

Cameron finally stopped glowering at Ian. Maybe he didn't like her partner either. That had to suck to not like your own employee. When she was alive, she had times when just being nice to her fellow workers was tough.

"Holly has stopped her deep mourning thanks to the spirit guides I sent to her last Christmas, but she has failed to join the living. She goes to work and does her errands, but beyond that, she stays by herself. It's become worse with the Christmas season." Cameron paused. "It's critical that she begin to socialize again."

Ian nodded, but Coco wanted more. "If your wife has stopped her mourning, why is she not socializing? Do you know? That might help us with our approach."

"I believe it's because she doesn't want to intrude on other people's lives. She thinks everyone else has the perfect life. Also, people who have come into our shop have shown her pity and she hates that."

Coco could hear the pride in Cameron's voice. Rumors around

the lounge had it that Cameron and Holly had one of those rare loves that only happen to one in a hundred couples. She'd seen many perfectly matched couples both while alive and in her new existence. If what her boss and his wife had once had was even better than that then she would do whatever it took to help Holly.

She glanced at Ian. He remained absolutely still, staring at Cameron. Did the man have no reaction? No feelings? His appearance seemed to grow more distinct, intense. She blinked. Nope. He was still a hard statue.

When she looked back at her boss, he was studying her, but he quickly moved his attention to Ian. "Do you have any questions?"

"Yes, one." He paused and spared her a brief look. "If you have Coco, who is quite capable of handling a case, then why do you need me to accompany her?"

Her mouth dropped open in astonishment. Was that a compliment from "Mr. Holier Than Thou"? The man did nothing but argue with her about anything and everything when they came into accidental contact with each other. Now he complimented her?

Cameron's mouth had opened and closed a couple times before he gave voice to his thoughts. "Coco, if you wouldn't mind, I'd like to talk to Ian alone."

She rose. "Of course. I'll drop in and see how Holly is." She looked at Ian. "If you are still on the case, just find me when you're ready."

"He will still be on the case." Cameron's hard tone sent a shiver down her spine. He was an easy going boss, not like her last one, but he did have a certain tone that made a person want to hightail it out of his office.

"Great." She didn't mean the word in any way, but she also didn't want to piss off Cameron. Phasing, she floated down through the floor, anxious to meet the woman who had captured her boss's heart.

Chapter Two

Ian's gut rolled into a sturdy knot at Cameron's tone. Fuck. He'd been muddling along just fine in his afterlife up until now. The last thing he wanted to do was partner on a case with Coco.

Besides her curvy figure and hypnotizing amber eyes, her energy pulled at him like quicksand. When she threw her dark brown hair with the pink streak over her shoulder and flashed one of her brilliant smiles, he wanted to grab her to him and kiss her until they both lost consciousness from lack of air—if that were possible as a spirit. But to do that meant to feel again.

Feeling was out of the question.

"Ian." Cameron's voice had lost its edge.

There may be a way out of this after all. "Yes."

"Have a seat."

Needing to negotiate his release from the case, he acquiesced to set the right mood.

Cameron came around his desk and sat on the edge of it. "Complimenting Coco won't get you out of this assignment."

He raised his brow. "That was not my intent. I was simply stating a fact. A fact that would negate the need for me to accompany her."

His supervisor shook his head. "This is not about her capabilities. There's a good chance she may run into difficulties while on this case, and I need you there as back up…and you may just learn something about yourself."

Discover something about himself? He snorted quietly. There was nothing he didn't already know, and what he knew, he didn't like. "I thought this was about your wife?"

Cameron's face softened. "It is." He stood and stared down at him. "And it better not get messed up or there will be consequences."

Ian straightened his shoulders. "I don't intend to make any mistakes." He was good at what he did. The question was, how was he supposed to perform well with another spirit watching him? And not just any spirit. "If, as you say, you need two spirits, then perhaps a spirit other than myself would be more appropriate."

Cameron stiffened.

Ian braced himself. Making his supervisor angry wasn't the smartest action he could have taken, but then again, he was well used to being on the receiving end of disapproval. His father had made him an expert.

But Cameron didn't yell at him. Instead, the man put a hand on his shoulder. "I know you don't want to do this, but you have to. Only by combining yours and Coco's talents can my wife come to see that not all is as it appears."

A strange sense of peace filled Ian's soul at Cameron's touch and he stood up, dislodging the hand on his shoulder. "You are incorrect. I am happy to do whatever is required of me. Is there anything else I should know?"

"Yes." Cameron's hazel eyes turned almost green. "You cannot fail."

"I don't plan to."

Coco floated into the One of a Kind Christmas Shop and scanned the people inside from where she hovered near the peaked ceiling. The joyful demeanors of those below filled her heart with warmth.

After a cursory review, it was clear no young children ran about the shop. The noise level was a happy muted tone as if the decorations for purchase were to be highly valued. She was pleased the residents of Deervale took Cameron and Holly's shop so seriously. It was such a wonderful idea. Anything bought there and given to a special someone would be precious, simply because it was one of a kind.

Though there were a few couples shopping, none had the intense golden glow of soulmates, but she'd become used to that when she was alive. At first, it had saddened her to know that people had married who weren't soulmates, but as she aged, she understood that not everyone found a soulmate and yet could live a very happy life.

Cameron's wife stood behind the counter, giving an older woman her change. Holly had a silver glow instead of a golden one. Her life of happiness had been cut short by Cameron's death. She didn't even look thirty years-old. She was of medium build, of a little less weight than Coco, and on the short side.

Her dark brown hair, which was held away from her face by the Santa hat she wore, brushed her shoulders and her smile lit up her round face, showing off a cute dimple in her right cheek. Round brown eyes sparkled with Christmas cheer as she spoke. "Thank you, Mrs. Bell. I hope your great niece loves that teddy bear ornament."

The older lady's smile faltered. "I wish I could see her open it, but my brother won't be visiting this year and I have so much baking to do."

Holly patted the woman's hand. "I can't believe you will be baking on Christmas day. It's just a train ride to London."

"Oi, it's much more than that—a drive to Edinburgh and then arrangements for them to pick me up, then the drive to Wembley.

No, it's much easier to stay here in my own home and my own comfy bed." Mrs. Bell winked.

"Are you going somewhere for Christmas dinner? I hope after all the cooking and baking you've done for others this year, that you were invited."

Mrs. Bell waved her off. "Oh, don't worry about me, young woman. I'm fine. Now I'd best go as I need to wrap this and box it so I can post it today."

Coco floated closer to Holly, curious to see her reaction.

Holly called out to Mrs. Bell, but the older woman was either hard of hearing or she didn't want Holly to ask her any more questions.

Holly muttered under her breadth. "You sly old woman. You have nowhere to go, do you?" She turned back toward her counter and smiled at the next customer.

Coco grinned at Holly's observation. She could definitely see why Cameron fell in love with her.

"What are you smiling about?" Ian floated down from the ceiling, but remained a little higher than she was. His rigid bearing, broad shoulders and height, probably intimidated many a spirit. But not her.

She shrugged. "Why not? It's Christmas time in a Christmas shop. You should try it."

Ian frowned.

She shook her head. "You're doing it wrong. The corners of your mouth are supposed to move up, not down."

Ian's mouth didn't move an inch, but he did raise a brow. "I'm sure you've deduced that we will be working together on this case since I'm here. For your sake, I did attempt to convince our supervisor that someone else might be more appropriate."

"My sake?" She floated higher so she could look him in the eye. "Why for my sake?"

The man's right eyebrow went even higher. Did he ever get it stuck up there?

"I am perfectly aware that you would rather accomplish this assignment with anyone other than myself."

Was she that obvious? "It's not that—"

Ian raised his hand. "Please, don't lie to spare my feelings. I'm not happy about this situation either."

She closed her mouth. First, she felt sorry for the bastard and then she wanted to smack him. "What I was about to say was that the real problem is we don't agree on how to handle our assignments, so this will be difficult at best. In fact, I bet you came here to counsel me on 'spying' on my charge before Cameron enables her to see us." She cocked her head. "Am I right?"

He nodded solemnly. "You are correct. However, I do think I have a solution."

Oh, this she couldn't wait to hear. "Yes?"

Ian floated a little higher. She wasn't sure if he did on purpose or just wasn't paying attention. She'd lay odds he knew exactly what he did.

He lowered his voice as if the living below them could hear. "I suggest we take turns. We both greet Holly on Christmas Eve, and then you can take the first visit and I'll take the next and back and forth."

Oh, she liked that idea. But her gut said Cameron wouldn't be happy, and she was far too curious about what visits Ian planned simply from reading the case file. And truth be told, if she agreed to his proposal, she'd end up spying on him anyway. She was nosy like that. "I do like your idea…"

Ian's shoulders seemed to lose some of their tension, which made her that much more curious about what his real motivation was. That, in itself, helped her make the decision.

"But I don't think Cameron would like it. He wants us to work together for Holly's sake, so if we keep our focus on her, I believe we can make this work." She'd guessed he wouldn't be happy with her reply, but she hadn't expected the almost panicked look that entered his gray eyes, lightening them before he turned away abruptly.

"Then I will see you Christmas Eve."

"Wait, don't you want to see how Holly interacts now, so we can better figure out which visits will work?" He wouldn't stay, but she was too interested in seeing his face again.

He shook his head and spoke over his shoulder. "No. I will ascertain all I need to know from the file." Without another word, he floated through the ceiling of the shop and out the roof.

She could follow him, insist on more conversation, but it probably wouldn't do any good. Though she had to work with the 'ice man,' as a few of the other spirits called him, her main focus had to stay on Holly. She turned around to see what her charge was up to.

A teenage boy approached the counter. He was at that age between boy and man, his limbs just a little too long for his body with an exuberance for life that came with being young and healthy. She'd guess he was in high school as she'd call it in Kentucky, but the Scots would call it secondary school. She'd done a little research before dropping in on Holly, one of the advantages of being able to travel through time easily.

Interesting that Cameron had never assigned her to another country. Not that it mattered, though she did have a mild curiosity about who her own soulmate might be. While alive she was convinced it was someone from a foreign country or countries, but since she was dead, it really was a moot point. She didn't see any soulmate glows among the spirits in the afterlife. Only among the living.

The teenager spoke to Holly. "Good afternoon, Mrs. Douglas. Do you think this would be a good present for my girlfriend? She likes to play netball."

"Good afternoon, Luca. This doesn't sound like the ballet dancer you were dating last Christmas."

Luca handed the ornament over. "No, it isn't. I had to dump the other one. We had irreconcilable differences."

Coco laughed but Holly held her countenance, barely. Coco was pretty sure the woman bit the inside of her cheek to keep from laughing. She definitely liked Holly.

"I see." Holly picked up the glass butterfly and studied it. "I'm not sure, Luca. If she likes playing sports, this might be more delicate than she cares for. Did you see the wood carved ornaments of sports equipment in the back corner?"

"But you said last year that I couldn't go wrong with something pretty and dainty."

Holly came around the counter. "That was true for your last girlfriend, but a present should reflect the person you're giving it to. Let me show you these other ornaments."

As Holly led Luca toward the back of the store, Coco floated upward, a plan already forming in her mind for Holly, and another for Ian.

She hadn't wanted to work with him, but now her curiosity was aroused and she looked forward to their next discussion.

Ian threw the case file on the redwood burl coffee table. That was perfectly useless. Cameron obviously didn't want them to know anything about his wife. That made depending on the case file for determining visits difficult. It also made Coco right, and that wasn't something he planned to admit.

He'd already miss-stepped by complimenting her. At least she and Cameron thought it was because he wanted off the case. That was, in fact, true, but he wasn't completely oblivious to the other spirit guides. Coco was one of the exceptional ones. He had no doubt that her success was based on instinct and warmth. It was the latter that scared the shit out of him.

Having solidified the moment he'd entered Kilkerran Hall, his family estate, he strode from the living room, past the formal dining room, and into the kitchen. It would have been faster to float to the kitchen for a beer or simply wish for the ale he preferred, but he wanted to walk off his tension. He hated feeling unsettled.

Opening the commercial-sized refrigerator, he grabbed two ales then pulled a bottle opener from a nearby drawer before he continued into his study. Prying off the top of one bottle, he set the other on his desk and sat back in his leather chair.

He took a swig. He had no doubts as to why he'd been made a spirit guide. Unlike Coco, who had clearly been open to her fellow man, woman and child while alive, he had not. He was here to atone for his mistakes, and based on his life, as short as it had been, he would be here forever, existing in his empty family home and working off his sins.

He rubbed his thumb along the side of the bottle neck, the condensation dripping onto the polished wood floor. There was only one significant difference between his existence while alive and now. Unfortunately, that very difference was about to become known and when it did, expectations would be raised and he'd fail miserably…again.

He closed his eyes as memories seeped into his brain in snapshots, unwelcome and unwanted. Ella, beautiful in her wedding dress, her eyes closed forever as the mortician secured the lid of the casket. The sting of her mother's hand as it connected with his cheek. Her younger brother, granted a leave from university, staring daggers at him even as Ella's dad ushered his family out into the parking lot.

He'd deserved it all and more.

Opening his eyes, Ian took another swig of ale. He deserved his new assignment, too. The afterlife had been too easy. He'd been assigned children since he'd arrived, all of them giving him the warmth he craved but in a safe place, on the living plane.

Now he would have to contend with Coco while helping his supervisor's wife. As if one set of stakes wasn't high enough, Cameron had compounded them. Ian would wager Remiel had a lot to do with that, finally pushing him into his real punishment.

He finished the ale and set the empty bottle on his desk. Scratching the left side of his chest where his cross tattoo covered his heart, he stared at the painting across the room. Picking up the other ale, he saluted it. "To your peace, wherever you are."

Tipping the bottle, he chugged the amber liquid until there was nothing left. Then he stood and threw it across the room where it shattered against the marble fireplace. The brief satisfaction he enjoyed over the broken glass would be gone in an instant, yet every time he had an ale, he did it again. A pathetic rebellion at best.

Now it appeared he was forced to "spy" on Holly Douglas. Everything inside him shuddered at lowering himself to such a level, but there was no help for it. Better to get it over with.

Instantly, he phased and floated through the roof of Kilkerran Hall. Though he could be at the One of a Kind Christmas Shop in Deervale in the blink of an eye, he took his time flying over the short distance from his family home near Crosshill to the small town, once known for its lace, now known for its music festival.

Another perk of the afterlife, the ability to float and fly at whim was not lost on him, not to mention the freedom to step through time.

There were few rules in his current existence and they were easy to follow. The consequences of ignoring them far outweighed any small inconvenience they may engender. Not solidifying while on the living realm was the most important, but there were a few more.

Slipping through the roof of the small Christmas shop, Ian scanned the area for Coco before looking for his assignment. Since she wasn't there, he breathed easier and focused on Mrs. Douglas.

After observing her a few moments, he concurred with Cameron, she had conquered her deep grief and her smiles at her customers were genuine. He floated closer to listen to her conversation.

"I think it's a great idea to buy the ornament *you* want to add to the tree, Sophia. After all, no one knows your taste like you do."

The tall woman with a long face and bright red straight hair to her shoulders, smiled condescendingly. "Exactly. Now I need to get home and find the perfect place to hang it on my tree."

"Merry Christmas!" Holly called after Sophia who was already halfway out the door.

No sooner had that customer left than two more came in. "There she is. I told you, Sarah, she can't escape us as long as she keeps this shop."

Ian watched as a man with a similar build to Cameron's, but with light brown hair, strode behind the counter and gave Holly a bear hug. It had to be Brody Hamilton. He and a man named Ethan Stewart were Cameron's two best friends, but the file said that Brody was a force to be reckoned with.

The woman watching the hug, smiled kindly. That must be Sarah Gowan, Brody's fiancée. Sarah was blonde and svelte and when Brody finally released Cameron's widow, she stepped in to give her a kiss on the cheek and a gentle embrace.

He was pleased to see Holly was still friends with them. That meant his task of coaxing her into daily life again would be that much easier.

"So Holly, we are here to invite you to our annual Christmas Eve party. You are coming, aren't you?" Brody raised an eyebrow high as if his question was rhetorical.

"You have to say yes this year." Sarah put her hand on Holly's arm. "You can't leave me alone with all his 'uni' friends."

Holly laughed. "I happen to know that there will be at least a half dozen women there to protect you from Brody's university buddies."

"How do you know that?"

With her finger, Holly pushed a laser cut wood ornament of a cardinal that hung on a display near the counter and sent it swinging back and forth. "Let's just say a little birdie told me."

Brody laughed and pulled Sarah to his side. "Don't you know, dove? Holly Douglas' shop is the place where all the gossip is spread." He looked at Holly. "You don't believe all that bull—"

"Brody." Sarah hissed even as she covered his mouth. "It's the Christmas season. Behave."

He winked at her. "Or St. Nicholas won't bring me any presents?"

"More like Mrs. Nicholas won't bring you the special gift she has for you."

Brody's smile disappeared. "Oh, not that. I promise to behave."

Sarah rolled her eyes. "That will last about two minutes."

Holly laughed, obviously enjoying the byplay between the couple. She appeared comfortable and relaxed, so why wasn't she socializing with these people? Cameron said she needed to learn that not all was as it appeared.

"If I have to behave, then you must come to our party." Brody's smile was weak as if he knew he pushed her toward a place she wasn't ready to go yet.

"Thank you. I'll see."

"What? Are you saying you have a better invitation than ours?" Brody widened his eyes in shock.

Holly chuckled even as she shook her head. "No, but that is my busiest day and Mr. Branson always comes in at the last minute without fail. I usually have barely enough energy to walk next door and fall into bed."

The man gave her a look of disbelief, but then a genuine smile graced his face. "I know it's hard, but we would really like you to come. It's not the same without you."

Holly lost her smile. "It's not the same without Cam either. Let me see how I feel."

Brody opened his mouth, but Sarah grasped his arm, beating him to a response. "That's all we ask. Just know that we will set a place for you."

Holly smiled in relief. "Thank you."

Brody turned to Sarah, love shining in his gaze. "Did you need to look for any last minute gifts while we're here?"

Sarah shook her head. "No, I was done shopping weeks ago, wasn't I, Holly?"

Holly nodded. "That's right. You told me so when you were here picking up that final item." Holly winked, her tension at being asked to the party having dissipated as they backed off.

"Okay then. We'll let you get back to your customers." Brody glanced toward the man next in line before smiling a goodbye.

"Wait." Holly moved from behind the counter and pulled Sarah and Brody away from the other shoppers. She lowered her voice, so Ian floated closer. "I do know someone who loves people and has no invitation for Christmas Eve."

Sarah touched Holly's arm. "Who?"

"Mrs. Bell."

Brody's eyebrows lifted in surprise. "I can't believe it. With all the cooking she does for others? Then we must ask her."

Sarah nodded. "Let's stop by her cottage on the way home."

Brody laughed. "Sarah, she lives in the opposite direction."

"Oh, I know that. But we must convince Mrs. Bell that we were out and about, and she was on the way home."

Brody squeezed Sarah around the waist and looked at Holly. "See why I love her?"

Holly nodded before looking back at the growing line. "I

better go. Thank you for the invitation." No sooner had she finished speaking then she hurried back to the counter with a smile.

Ian vaguely wondered if Brody and Sarah's relationship was not all it appeared or if they could skip that visit.

"She's amazing, isn't she?"

Ian whipped around at the voice behind him.

Coco floated there in a festive red corduroy dress that accentuated her bustline with its square neckline. It completely covered her arms in a loose long sleeve and flared out at her knees. She looked good enough to eat until his gaze flew back to the plaid sash on her shoulder.

The Fergusson tartan. What the fuck? He frowned. "Why are you tailing me and why are you wearing my clan tartan?"

The soft look on Coco's face after witnessing Holly's kindness disappeared faster than a peregrine falcon bent on its prey. Her amber eyes glittered with irritation. "First of all, I wasn't tailing you like you were some common criminal. I'm sure your crimes would be anything but common."

That hit far too close to home for comfort.

"I was looking for you so we could agree on a plan and start our assignment."

She took a breath, probably to calm herself more than because she needed air to continue. "Second of all, I dressed for the festivities of bringing Holly to visit her neighbors and family. This is not an uncommon outfit to wear to a ceilidh and since I have no clan and you are my partner, when it came to the choice of tartan, it made sense to show Holly a united front by wearing the same plaid you do."

She stopped and looked him over from his tan slacks to his dark blue golf shirt. "You haven't changed."

"I was unaware it was a requirement."

"Are you telling me you wear the same clothes for every

assignment?" Her look of incredulity struck him as humorous, but he kept that to himself.

"Yes."

She opened her mouth and closed it several times, but didn't actually form any words.

"I don't think the children care what I'm wearing. I suppose I could dress like a clown, but I never liked clowns when I was young and had many friends who were in agreement with me. So rather than scare the youngsters, I dress simply."

"Wait. You have only been a spirit guide for children?" Her brow puckered with puzzlement.

"Yes."

She huffed. "Do you always answer questions with one word?"

He couldn't resist. "Yes."

She threw her hands up. "Seriously?"

His lip quirked slightly upward. "No."

She squinted her eyes at him. "You're playing with me, aren't you?" She placed her hands on her hips. "You better be playing with me because that is absolutely rude behavior if you're not."

He didn't say anything. Watching her was too enjoyable to spoil it by responding. The pink streak in her hair appeared to glow as she swung it over her shoulder. Even her cheeks were flushed.

"So how long have you been a spirit guide?"

He raised an eyebrow. "I believe you will recall there is no time in the afterlife."

"Yes, I do remember that fact. So how many cases have you completed?"

He shrugged. "I would estimate about two hundred and forty-seven."

She looked askance at him. "That's a guess?"

"Yes." He could have elaborated, but since his one word

answers threw her into such a passion, he couldn't resist making them. Not very sporting of him, but enjoyable nonetheless.

Her whole demeanor softened, taking him off guard. "I didn't know you were good with children. Cameron must have chosen you for that purpose."

He stiffened. She would discover more about him than anyone knew if he participated in this assignment, and the last thing he needed was for her to be gossiping about him with any spirit that might come into the lounge, her favorite place to retreat. "I cannot begin to fathom what's in Cameron Douglas' mind. I expect he found me to be more than competent when dealing with child assignments."

There went her pink streak again, back over her shoulder and her eyes flashed at him. "Do you always have to sound so stuffy? Seriously, you'd drive a saint to sin."

He raised his eyebrow. "Doubtful."

<h1 style="text-align:center">Chapter Three</h1>

Coco clamped her mouth shut to keep her growl of irritation from emerging. She'd known this assignment with Ian would be a pain in the neck, but it hadn't even begun yet and she was ready to strangle him.

Maybe she should focus on the assignment and mull over why Ian was assigned only children's cases later. "So you aren't going to change?"

He floated in front of her, again just slightly higher with his arms crossed over his chest. "No."

If she wasn't so fed up with him, she'd be admiring the way his biceps stretched the sleeves of his shirt to the max, but she was too irritated to truly appreciate his physique at the moment. "Then I suggest we discuss our plan. I've watched Holly, as did you and I think we should visit Brody, Sophia, Luca, and Mr. Branson's homes."

"No."

She stared at him, her mouth open because she was pissed off now. Throwing up her hands, she floated out of the shop and straight to Cameron Douglas' office.

She popped up through the floor only to see she'd interrupted him in a meeting with Joy, a spirit guide she admired greatly and tried to emulate, but her own temper was so hard to control. "I'm sorry. I'll come back later." She would just move through time.

Cameron nodded and she quickly adjusted her entrance to later. This time when she popped up from the floor, there was no one there but him.

He sat at the edge of his desk. "What do you need, Coco?"

She solidified and flopped into the closest chair. "He's impossible."

Cameron nodded. "I know, but I need him on this case. He's the only one who can complete the job, and it's as important to him as it is to me, though he doesn't know it yet."

"Then why do you need me?" So her voice sounded a little whiney. She was entitled after dealing with that arrogant asshole.

"Because he won't succeed without you."

"What?"

Cameron stood and put his hands on her shoulders. "I'm sorry I have to make you work with him. If I thought anyone else could handle him, I'd let you off the hook, but the fact is, you're the best spirit guide for the job. You won't let him walk all over you, but you'll listen to reason when he's reasonable."

She stared at her boss. Her heart jumped for joy because he recognized her abilities, but part of her was skeptical. "Why do I think you're just saying that to get your way?"

Cameron laughed, his brown hair falling onto his forehead again. "Ach, busted. Yes, I was laying it on a little thick, but it's still true. This is my wife, Coco. I need *you* to help her."

Her heart froze at the look of desperation that flashed in Cameron's hazel eyes, making them almost as gray as Ian's. "Only for you. But I reserve the right to come back here and vent."

Cameron stepped back, his face relaxing at her acceptance. "Anytime." He held up his hand. "And I even promise not to try and solve your problems with Ian. I'll just listen."

She stood herself. "Wow, Holly trained you well."

He grinned, but there was a faraway look in his eye. "Aye, she did."

His gruff voice made her feel as if she intruded on a private moment. She waited, not sure how she should respond. Finally, his gaze turned back to her. "I'll go see Holly now, prepare her so she can see you and Ian."

She grimaced. "Let me know when she's ready."

He nodded and she took that as her sign to leave. Quickly, she phased and slipped down through the floor. A part of her ached for what Cameron used to have. She'd always expected to find her soulmate, but she never had, and now it was too late.

Blinking her eyes to keep the tears at bay, she flew back to Holly's shop to find Ian. When she arrived, he wasn't there.

She fisted her hands in frustration. "Frick."

Holly stood at the door of her shop and looked out the window for the twentieth time in twenty minutes. "Come on, Mr. Branson, where are you?"

Every year, he came right at five on Christmas Eve as she was locking the door, and she had to wait until half past for him to choose just the right ornament for his wife. They had been married forever and last year he chose a singing cardinal with flapping wings. He said it was perfect because it moved just like his wife did since he'd bought her a new scooter. If the truth were told, Mrs. Branson hadn't stopped moving since that day.

Last year, Holly hadn't minded because she had no one to go home to. Cameron was gone and she was alone. The years before that she didn't mind because she and Cam worked together until they closed. But last year everything changed when Cameron came to visit her on Christmas Eve.

The closer Christmas came this year, the happier she felt. She'd been preparing everything—the decorations in their home next door, how she would dress, what she would say. Her heart ached for him every day, but the spirits he sent last year had shown her how lucky she'd been to know a love like theirs and to cherish it.

Of course, she'd helped them just as much, and that was one reason she felt confident Cameron would return this year.

She walked into her office in the back and shut out the light, the small snowman night-light the only glow in the room. While she was excited to see Cameron again, there was a small part of her that was curious as to how he would want her to help him this year. She was certain that if she kept doing a good job with his spirit workers, he'd keep coming back to see her every year.

It wasn't the same as still having him with her, but it was so much better than not ever seeing him again. She shivered at the thought of her first year without Cam. This year between the happy memories Duncan and Jessica had reminded her of, and more that had come back, she'd made it through.

She walked back into the shop and moved to the counter to tidy it up. Of course, knowing her hunky late husband would be visiting her on Christmas Eve had been another motivator to stop crying every night. A lot of her anger over Cameron dying on her had dissipated. It may not be gone completely, but had definitely taken a back burner to her anticipation.

She looked at the clock on the wall. It was five past. She really should lock the door and head next door to eat, shower, and dress. She walked toward it, balking at the idea of Mr. Branson not being able to buy his wife his annual Christmas ornament. The older man didn't get around as easily as his wife. He used a cane and limped along as best he could.

Not seeing him in the street, she moved around the shop, straightening out the decorations on shelves and readjusting the ornaments on the large tree in the center of the main room. Having the high ceiling of many of the buildings on main street, she and

Cameron had bought the fifteen-foot tree to hold many of their one-of-a-kind ornaments.

She smiled. They'd outgrown that tree by their second year and added four additional smaller trees as well as display racks.

At the sound of the bell at the door, she spun around to see Mr. Branson limp inside. "Mr. Branson, I'd almost given up on you."

The older man gave her half a smile. "I don't move as quickly as I used to."

"Well, that's fine. I'm still here. Is there anything in particular you were looking for this year?"

Mr. Branson shrugged. "No. I'll know it when I see it."

She watched as he hobbled toward the large tree. His limp was much more pronounced. Maybe it was time he bought himself a scooter. "How long have you been married, Mr. Branson?"

He mumbled from the side of the tree. It sounded like he said "forever." That had to be her imagination. She walked over to where he'd stopped to peruse a set of ceramic mouse ornaments, all hand painted.

"How long did you say?"

He glanced at her. "Sixty years this past June. Of course, we married when I was five and she three."

She chuckled. "Ah, so that's the true meaning of the term child-bride."

He nodded before returning to his search.

She glanced at the clock again. She had time. It was very important for Mr. Branson to have the time to choose just the right gift for his wife of more than sixty years. They were so lucky to still have each other.

She walked back to the counter to allow him to look. He might take even more than his usual 30 minutes to find an ornament considering how slow he moved now. He had to be at least seventy-eight.

"I'll take this one." Mr. Branson called from the back of the tree.

She was about to go look as she was shocked he would decide on something so quickly, when she heard him shuffling toward her. She immediately pulled out a gift box since he always had her wrap it.

When he handed over the ornament and the pounds needed to pay for it, her surprise compounded. It was a mouse sitting under a mushroom and on his lap was a tiny present. She remembered unwrapping it from the shipment and thinking it would never sell. Instead of a smile of anticipation on the little mouse, his face was wistful.

She looked Mr. Branson in the eye. "Are you sure? That was quick."

"I'm sure. This little guy spoke to me."

"Okay. Did you want that gift wrapped?"

The old man shook his head. "No, I've kept you too late as it is. Just put it in a sack."

Something in the tone of his voice struck her as sad. She hated to think he felt rushed. "Really, I don't mind." She held a piece of wrapping up to show her willingness.

"Ach, no. I wasn't even expecting you to be open and almost went straight home, so I think I can take it in a sack."

"Very well." She wrapped the mouse in tissue and placed it in a bag. After giving him the change, she walked him to the door. "You have a Merry Christmas."

He looked at her and patted her arm. "No, my dear. *You* have a Merry Christmas." Then he hobbled out onto the dark street.

She couldn't shake the feeling that Mr. Branson wasn't his usual self, but since his wife had been in not two days earlier talking up a storm and hadn't mentioned any ill health on his part, Holly could only shrug and lock the door.

She immediately flipped the switch on the lights, which also switched off every Christmas bulb and moving ornament, another smart idea of Cam's.

Lastly, she turned off the lights that surrounded the sign proclaiming it the One of a Kind Christmas Shop and made her way around the ceramic ornament display to the tapestry that hid the door to her home on the other side of the wall.

Stepping into her house, she turned on the lights. "Mac, what are you doing up there?"

The large gray cat met her gaze with its golden one then looked down and batted a plastic sheep off the side table in the living room.

Holly strode toward the cat. "I wasn't *that* late. You'd think you missed me or something."

The cat batted another sheep onto the floor before lying across the entire table sending plastic sheep, camels, and donkeys scattering. Mac was part Scottish fold, part who knew what, so his folded ears that made him look apologetic didn't fool her.

She picked up the fifteen-pound bundle of attitude and gave him a hug. "Hmmm, I missed you too, you big lug." She set him on the floor where he proceeded to rub himself against her legs.

"What do you have against these sheep?" She knelt down to gather up the plastic figures.

Mac decided he needed to get involved and pushed them around like he was playing American soccer. "Excuse me. You could at least help."

As she reached for the final piece, Mac batted it under the sofa.

Holly sat on her haunches. "Really?"

Laughter behind her had her twisting around, even as she pressed her hand to her chest as if it could slow her suddenly racing heart. "Holy crap, you scared me!"

Her late husband, Cameron Douglas, floated by the Christmas tree in his usual blue, green and white Douglas kilt, looking more handsome than the day she met him. She stayed where she was as she gazed at him, overwhelmed to actually see him again.

His hazel eyes sparkled with mirth and his smile was wider than the Atlantic. He wore a loose peasant shirt as if he were dressed for a ceilidh. He never did wear the formal attire except at their wedding.

"Love, I know you can still speak. I heard you talking to Mac."

At the sound of his name, the cat rose from the floor where he lay after making his sofa goal and sauntered over to his dad.

Holly stared, jealous as the cat rubbed against Cam's legs before sitting on its haunches and staring up at him.

"Holly?" Cam's smile disappeared as he gazed at her with love and concern. "You did remember I would visit you, right?"

She shook her head to clear it. "Of course." She rose on shaky legs. "I've been looking forward to it all year. I wasn't expecting you until—Oh."

He floated closer. "What is it?"

All her planning was ruined. "I wasn't ready for you. I haven't even turned on the lights of the Christmas tree. Oh, and I was going to change into what I bought to wear just for you."

"You know I'm just happy to see you." His smile came back, but a softer one than before.

She could feel his love. Too full of joy at seeing him to let her disappointment ruin it, she nodded. "I love you, Cam."

"I know, hen. I love you, too."

"I wish I could touch you." She stepped forward and raised her hand to his cheek, but it went right through him. Her frustration brought tears to her eyes. To wait all year, even knowing she couldn't touch him, was still torture.

He raised his hands as if he would take her by the shoulders and pull her in for an embrace, but at the last minute he linked them behind his head, causing his hair to fall forward onto his forehead.

"I know you do, but this is all that I can do. It's supposed to make you happy."

She smiled even as she wiped her eyes with the back of her hand, hating her tears for blurring her sight. "I am."

Cam chuckled. "Last I knew, tears were for sadness."

She straightened her shoulders, determined to be strong so she could be with him for as long as possible. "I'm fine. A year is a long time to wait, but I'm really happy you're here." She widened her smile, wanting more than anything that he would stay the night.

"I'm glad because I need your help again." Cam floated over to the electric fireplace. With him on the other side of the room, Mac jumped into her comfy chair, his bed since last year when he forced her to take Cam's.

"Is it more spirit employees? How are Jessica and Duncan?" She'd enjoyed her time with the Spirits of Christmas Past last year.

Cam grinned. "They're great. No more worries for those two, but the two this year will be tough."

She sat on the arm of Cam's chair, unable to take her eyes off him. "Why? What do you need me to do?"

"I need to help them build common ground. They've never worked together and have opposite views on everything." Cam rolled his eyes. "I would never put these two together, but it's important that they learn to get along."

She gave her husband a shrewd look. "Are you matchmaking?"

He looked startled. "If I were, these are the last two I would put together. He's a Scottish millionaire, family money, and she's from Kin-tuckey and managed an ice cream shop."

Holly laughed. "It's Kentucky. You make it sound funny with your accent."

"I thought you loved my accent." He gave her puppy dog eyes, which caused her to laugh more.

"I do. It's all part of your Scottish charm. Maybe your Scottish spirit will charm your Kentucky one. Can you tell me their names so I don't have to talk about them based on where they're from?"

"Right. The Scotsman is Ian Fergusson."

"The rich one."

He nodded. "And the American woman is Coco Baker."

"Ouch." Holly grimaced. "Did her mother really name her Cocoa Baker as in hot chocolate?"

Cameron's forehead crinkled in puzzlement until understanding dawned. "I hadn't thought of that."

Holly sighed. "Men."

Cameron floated closer. "No, your man."

Her breath hitched. "And I'm your woman forever."

Cameron gazed into her eyes. "Yes, forever…" He blinked. "But that shouldn't keep you from living a full life until we are together again."

She cocked her head. "Don't worry, I am."

His look told her he didn't agree, but he didn't say anything. Relieved he wouldn't push the issue, she glanced at the clock. "So are you here early so we can spend more time together?"

She wanted to tell him all about her year. The shop had done well even through the third quarter, far surpassing any year they'd had so far. And she'd—

"I'm afraid not, hen. As much as I want to spend more time with you, I can't. I risk turning into a ghost and you know what would happen then."

Disappointed, she nodded. "You would haunt me every day but when I passed, you'd be stuck here while I moved on."

"That's right, love."

"But it's so long to wait. Sometimes I wish I could—"

"No!" Cameron swooped to her so fast she stepped back in surprise. "Don't think like that. Promise me you will live every day fully and completely. Promise me you will be patient."

He was so close she could see the stormy gray in his hazel eyes glowing with his intensity. He truly believed she might want to end her life early. She hated to admit that the thought had occurred, but she'd pushed it away. "I promise. I know how precious life is, even if I can't have you for all these years I thought we'd have."

Stark pain flashed in his eyes before he turned away. "I know. I'm sorry. Our separation is my fault, and I will pay for it until we are reunited." He turned to face her again. "But until that time, we both have things we must do and we must do them well."

She gave him half a smile. "You mean like help two spirits get along."

"Yes. But also you must live life to the fullest, not just in the shop."

Crap. "Have you been watching me?"

"I don't have to watch you to know. For now, focus on Ian and Coco. We can talk about the rest later."

"So you'll come back after they leave, just like last year."

He grinned. "St. Nick himself couldn't keep me away."

Warmth spread through her chest at the love she felt coming from him. "Excellent! Now let me turn the lights on. I purchased some very special ornaments because I knew you would see them." She rose from the arm of his chair.

"I can't." He started to float upwards.

"Why? It will only take a minute. You must have more time. It's not even half past seven." The need to keep him there made her desperate.

"I'm sorry, love. I have to go. Our connection is too strong."

"But you'll come back tonight, right? Promise me." Her voice rose in pitch, revealing her panic, but she couldn't help it.

"Aye, I promise." He blew her a kiss as he neared the ceiling. "I love you, hen."

"I love you, t…" She watched as he disappeared through the

roof. Running to the front door, she quickly unlocked it and ran out into the street, looking for any sign of Cam above their house, but he was gone.

She crossed her arms over her chest at the cold and looked down the empty main road of Deervale. Lights from inside homes between the dark shops sent squares of glowing light into the street, which made the insides appear even warmer. As she walked back to her house, she heard laughter across the road and her spirits sank.

She'd waited all year for Cam to appear and in less than thirty minutes he was gone. Resentment filled her, and her anger at him for dying in the first place built.

When she reached her open door, Mac sat on the sill staring at her. "What? Don't look at me like that. Get your butt back inside."

He turned and ran, listening to her for once.

Ian walked into the lounge and scanned it for Coco. It wasn't hard to find her. Her wide smile and flashing eyes would catch anyone's attention. He couldn't believe every other spirit in the room wasn't staring at her, but they weren't. Some were drinking at the bar. Others were painting landscapes and another group of spirits were completely engrossed in a card game.

She sat on a couch with Mrs. Ferrisletter, an older woman from 1662 London who served as one of the trainers for spirit guides. Maybe Coco needed extra advice for how to handle Holly Douglas' case. She could have simply asked him.

He thought back to their last conversation. Maybe not. They didn't exactly concur on the best plan of action.

Coco caught sight of him and her smile left. He did tend to have that effect on people. She rose, then bent over and gave the older woman a hug.

Ian's body reacted completely inappropriately. Her rounded ass caused the bottom of her dress to flare wide, so he moved his gaze to a painting on the wall. Unfortunately, it was a Ruben, and it was the one of The Three Graces, which meant three naked full figured women and one with her back to him.

What the fuck was that doing there?

"I take it you heard from Cameron?"

He jerked his attention from the painting to her face. His gaze was immediately drawn to what looked like a candy cane adhered to her skin just to the side of her right eye. He had the almost uncontrollable urge to lick it.

Stepping back, he took a calming breath. What was the matter with him? "Yes."

She looked at the ceiling for a long moment. In fact, for so long that he glanced upward to see if there was something there to be seen, but there was nothing besides the pale pink sky with naked cupids flying among clouds.

He frowned. He didn't remember those being up there. Then again, he rarely came to this area. Too many spirits relaxed here.

"Ian. Ian."

Her voice had him redirecting his gaze. "Yes?"

"I'm setting some ground rules. First one is, if you answer a question with only the word 'no,' you will be expected to explain. If you answer it with 'yes,' I will let it slide. Agreed?"

He didn't deserve to have this kind of fun. He'd been so focused on how to hide who he was from Coco, he hadn't anticipated how much enjoyment he might have with her around. The intellectual stimulation of countering her expectations alone would be a pleasure.

"So are we agreed?" She stared defiantly up at him, her gaze fully on him.

He waited an extra second. "Yes."

"Grrr." Coco brushed by him after her growl.

He barely held back his grin. The woman actually growled, and that deep sound had sent his blood rushing to his groin. He remained where he was, regaining control of his body, when it occurred to him that this might very well be more of his punishment.

He'd known that Coco's vitality attracted him like a salmon to its nesting ground, but now to discover he wanted her sexually was the icing on the cake. He shook his head. How much could a spirit endure?

"Are you coming or not?" Her voice behind him had him turning.

He strode toward her. "After you."

She led the way, floating them down toward Holly's home.

He could maintain his silence, but the urge to keep Coco off balance was too strong. "Did Mrs. Ferrisletter have any sage counsel to impart?"

She stopped in mid-flight. "If you mean did I ask her for advice, the answer is no."

He raised his eyebrow, anxious to hear exactly what she'd been talking about if only to be entertained.

"No, she was asking me to think about being a spirit guide trainer."

He widened his eyes. "You?" It made perfect sense. Coco would be an excellent trainer. She liked spirits, was patient, and tended to get right to the heart of the matter.

Her hands found her hips. "Yes, me. Why not, me? I'm frickin' good at what I do."

Ian fully agreed, but he wouldn't let her know that. "I'm merely curious that there is an opening that needs to be filled of which I was unaware."

"Seriously? Of course you didn't know about it. You're never around. As it turns out, Duncan Montgomerie left on an assignment for Cameron to help Holly and didn't come back."

She leaned closer as if someone might overhear them in between space and time. "Neither did his brand new mentee. I think something went wrong and that's why Cameron is sending us. Whatever they were supposed to do, I think they failed and that's why he needs us."

He raised his brow at her deduction, but didn't say anything.

His silence didn't make her happy. She huffed and started them on their way again. "I don't know why I even try."

He didn't know either, but he was glad she did.

Chapter Four

They arrived in Holly's living room. Ian was struck by the hominess of it despite the cathedral ceiling and large size. The heavy set tree took up a large corner of the room. It appeared as wide as it was tall. There were two overstuffed chairs that had seen better days, one of which was occupied by a sleeping Holly Douglas and the other by a rather large gray cat, also sleeping. The electric fireplace was on the opposite side of the room from the tree, and the rest of the space was filled with small tables and bookshelves filled with Christmas décor.

At a quick glance, he noticed three manger scenes, two trains, both of which were running, a ski slope complete with a skiing Santa, and an entire Christmas village set up in the giant bay window.

"Wow, if there was a prize for the most Christmas spirit, Holly should get it." Coco once again leaned close as she whispered her observation.

This time, in the closeness of the room, he breathed in her scent. It was sweet and homey. He couldn't quite put his finger on it, but he liked it.

She pointed to the clock. She'd landed them just two minutes before midnight. That didn't surprise him. It was obvious she was ready to throw herself fully into their assignment.

He nodded in acknowledgment.

Obviously, he didn't hold her attention very long. She floated away from him to inspect the tree. He understood his lack of appeal, but it still bothered him. He followed her, keeping an eye on Holly. Since Cameron had already visited his wife, if she opened her eyes, she would see them.

It was then he noticed the cat watching them. It continued to lay with its head on its paws, but its gaze went back and forth between them. Cameron must have made it possible for the cat to see them as well. That was peculiar.

He tapped Coco on the shoulder.

"What?" She turned away from the miniature carousel going around and around as it hung from the tree.

He pointed to the cat. "Mac."

Coco's eyes widened and the tiny candy cane elongated. "Cameron made it possible for the cat to see us?"

He shrugged. "It appears so."

"That's strange." She floated closer to the gray beast and it sat up. With no fear whatsoever, she placed her hand over the cat as if to stroke it and she actually made contact.

Ian drew closer. That wasn't possible.

But the purring of the cat as Coco stroked it and scratched it behind the ears told him it was.

"I always wanted a cat, but mama said we couldn't afford to feed it. Then when I moved out, the landlord I rented from didn't allow pets." She sighed wistfully, which made him want to go out and buy her a cat immediately.

Once again, he floated away from her. He didn't like his strange reactions to her. On the other hand, if she could sway Holly as easily as she swayed him, their time together may be shorter than he anticipated.

The bongs of the grandfather clock announced the hour, and Coco floated back to stand beside him. He didn't know why, but he liked that. They could at least pretend to have a united front. Then again, if they were supposed to show Holly not all was as it appeared, she might see right through them.

At the last bong, Holly's eyes opened. She rubbed her eyes and yawned, then stretched before staring at them. "Spirits of Christmas Present, I presume." She smiled shyly, but she looked like a queen holding court with her rich red velvet robe draped regally around her and her forearms resting on the arms of the chair.

He bowed, playing to her pretend royalty, but Coco floated to her.

He shook his head behind Coco's back and grinned at Holly. She smiled back before turning her attention to Coco.

"Oh, I love your hair. I wonder if I could do something like that." Holly reached out to touch the pink streak and her hand went right through. "Oops, I forgot. I have to wait until you phase me."

Coco laughed. "I'm glad to see you are as anxious as I am. I'm Coco Baker. I'm from Kentucky originally. This gentleman is Ian Fergusson. He's from Scotland, not far from here actually."

She knew where he lived? His guard went up. What had she been doing? Researching him?

Holly looked at him. "I can't see you so well with all the flashing Christmas lights. Can you come closer?"

Coco moved to the side, allowing him to float in front of her. This made it easy for him to smile at Holly. "It's a pleasure to make your acquaintance."

Holly fanned herself. "Well, you do know how to make an impression, don't you?" She blushed prettily, her round cheeks taking on a rosy hue before her shy smile froze. "Wait, you look familiar. Have we met?"

His veins turned to ice in an instant. This was why he preferred children. He forced his smile wider. "I'm sure we haven't because if we had, I would have clearly remembered it." He winked for good measure.

Holly grinned. "Oh yes, if I'd met such a charmer before, I know I would have remembered you. I didn't mean to be rude, but one of my last spirits, Jessica, ended up being my very first case worker when I was still a teenager. Isn't that crazy?"

He nodded and floated back, his whole body colder than the Sound of Monach off the Outer Hebrides islands, which he'd fallen into in winter when he was a boy.

His family's life had always been covered in the tabloid newspapers. Some of the information was true and some wasn't, but the buggers reported his finance's death absolutely correct. He had no doubt that was where Holly had seen his face.

"Are you ready for your first visit?" Coco had her hand on Holly's shoulder.

Holly laughed. "I love the flying part. Where are we going? My family's house? Brody's? How much time is considered the present?"

Coco's eyes sparkled with excitement. "I think we should visit your family first, since you weren't able to get away to be with them."

At the mention of family, Ian joined them, kicking himself for not staying on task. "To answer your question about time, we have all of Christmas Eve and there are many places we need go." He gestured toward his partner. "Coco's right, your family is important, but before we do, I want to take you back just a few hours ago."

"Sounds like a plan to me." Holly slipped her hand into his, surprising him. He hadn't clasped hands with an adult since his early days with Ella.

Coco frowned at him as she took Holly's other hand. "Hold on tight. Ian will lead the way…on *this* visit."

He brought them through the bay window and into the quiet street.

"We're still here." Holly looked at him, her confusion clear.

"Watch your door." He pointed to her house with their clasped hands. "We've gone back to just about seven this evening."

There were still a few people walking briskly along the sidewalks. A cheery "Merry Christmas" sounded from down the street, while in the other direction they could hear a door open and new visitors being welcomed inside.

Coco, obviously impatient, sighed. "What are we waiting for?"

He shook his head at her and squeezed Holly's hand as a woman, a wee bit older than Holly, hesitated in front of her door. She pulled a paper out of her purse and studied it before looking at the numbers on Holly's house. Then she stepped next door and peered in the shop window.

"Ian, if you're trying to make me feel guilty for not staying open later, it's not going to work." Holly let go of Coco's hand and turned toward him. "Cam and I agreed on how late to stay open on Christmas Eve. We have a right to celebrate the holiday, too."

"But you don't *celebrate* the holiday, do you?" At her downcast look, he pointed again with their clasped hands. "But that's not what I'm showing you. Watch."

Her face filled with curiosity, Holly returned her attention to the woman who now walked back to Holly's house.

The woman raised her hand to knock, hesitated, then brought it back down. She stood staring at the door. A young couple approached and the woman moved back to the dark shop window.

"Does she want me to open the shop?"

He didn't answer. He didn't want to take Holly's attention from what was happening. Coco glared at him from behind Holly, so he shook his head again.

"Oh, she's going to knock. Wait for it." Holly's hand in his tightened as the woman moved back to Holly's door and raised her fist. She left it there for what must have been an entire minute before a cloud of frosty air escaped her slightly opened mouth and she stuffed her hand in her pocket.

Quickly, she turned and strode down the street. Holly pulled on his hand. "Come on, we have to follow her."

He floated them along, Coco bringing up the rear. He smirked. "Why do you want to know who she is?"

"Because she obviously wanted to talk to me then chickened out. I'm the easiest person to talk to, so it had to be something terrible."

"Why does it have to be something terrible, as you put it?" Sometimes the female brain was far more complicated than it needed to be.

Holly looked at him as if he were dense. "Ian, if it was good news, she would have knocked right away."

"I agree with Holly." Coco's voice sounded nervous. "It must be bad news, but the woman never knocked so Holly isn't supposed to know what it is."

He lowered his voice to imitate his father's. No one could resist anything his father said. "Holly needs to know."

"I do. My stomach is all in knots."

The woman stopped next to a Vauxhall Corsa parked on the side of the street and got in.

"Well, crap, now I'll never know."

Ian unclasped their hands. "Go ahead. Get inside. She's not leaving yet."

Holly's doubt warred with her need to satisfy her curiosity as she stared at him. "Okay."

As soon as she slipped into the car, Coco grabbed his arm. "Tell me. What will she find out?"

He covered her hand with his own, the warmth of her filling his soul, just as this tiny revelation to Holly would. He craved this. But he didn't deserve it. He released Coco's hand. "Watch for yourself."

"Seriously? You can be the most tight-lipped—"

"You're going to miss it."

His partner huffed and scowled at him before she slipped into the vehicle. He watched from outside. It had been sheer luck that he'd been in the street contemplating what visits Holly should make when the woman had approached her house. Like his female companions, he'd been curious, so he'd followed her.

Holly burst from the car. "Holy crap! I have a sister-in-law!" She floated in one place, a stunned expression on her face.

Coco phased through the vehicle to join Holly, putting an arm around her shoulders. "Did Cameron know he had a half-sister?"

Holly looked at him. "No. He said his parents both died shortly after he was born. He didn't even remember them, but his aunt and uncle raised him like their own. He even called them mom and dad and they threw us a big reception after we were married." Holly turned to Coco. "We eloped in Vegas because we had too many people on either side of the pond to force that kind of expense on one side."

"The pond?"

Holly smiled proudly at Coco. "That's what we call the Atlantic Ocean here in Scotland."

"I didn't know that." Coco smiled kindly. "So this woman has to have been born before Cameron's parents met or…"

Holly frowned. "Or one of Cam's parents was unfaithful. That would be so sad."

Coco glared at him for Holly's sad face.

He ignored her. "But now you know that there is part of Cameron's family that has searched you out. Did his uncle and aunt also ask you to share Christmas with them?"

Holly wouldn't look him in the eye. "I have the shop and they are way up in the highlands and the shop doesn't close until…"

He didn't say anything. She'd understood his point and that was all he wanted. He also wanted to present her with a new and exciting goal connected to Cameron. Finding her late husband's sister would force her to move beyond the walls of her shop and the grocery store.

"Talk about starting the evening off with a bang." Coco smiled, pulling Holly from her guilty silence. "I think the next stop should be with your family." She gave him an exasperated look. "If there are no objections to that."

He kept his grin to himself and waved his hand to the side. "As you see fit."

"As I see—?" She snapped her gaze to Holly. "Yes, if that works for you?"

Holly beamed. "I'd love to see my family. I haven't seen them since Cam died."

"What?" Coco took the word from his mouth.

Holly shrugged. "There was so much to do when he passed, and then I had to take over everything. When you're used to having two people to share the work, the change is pretty overwhelming."

"But you had family come for the funeral, right?" Coco's shock mirrored his own, but he was more irritated with Cameron for leaving so little in the case file and forcing them to discover it by accident. This was critical information for Holly's wellbeing.

"Oh yes." Holly answered Coco. "My mom and John came, and of course, the Tinders. Those are John's parents, but the rest of the family couldn't afford to come over."

"Then what are we waiting for?" Coco grasped Holly's hand.

Ian raised his own. "We are waiting for us to concur and I'm afraid I cannot condone a visit to America now."

"Excuse me?" Coco let go of Holly's hand and floated in front of him, her face level with his. "We followed your plan for the first visit. Now we follow mine."

"It's not about being fair to each of us." He looked over her shoulder at Holly, who had turned to watch Cameron's sister drive away. "It's about what will bring about a successful outcome for Holly."

"Ian Fergusson, if you think for one minute I'm buying that line of bullshit, you're sorely—"

Seeing no choice, he laid his hand on her shoulder and sped them to his family home.

"Mistak—" Coco sputtered to a stop as she took in her surroundings. Bookcases rose two stories high on every wall. From the ceiling hung not one, but three giant chandeliers and beneath her feet was what looked like the softest rug she'd ever seen. She immediately solidified to discover if she was right. She crouched and almost moaned at how silky the carpet was.

Ian was already solid and walking out of the room.

"Where are we?" She rose and followed him into a smaller room, but no less impressive. A marble fireplace dominated one side of it with a five-foot painting of a very stern, obviously wealthy man above it. Two large comfy looking recliners sat before the cold hearth.

The ceiling in this room was just as high but had no chandelier. It did have enormous windows that had to be fifteen feet tall at least. On the other side of the room was an eight-foot-wide mahogany desk, at least she thought it was mahogany as she'd never seen anything so big made out of it.

"I have root beer," Ian called from yet another room.

She hesitantly stepped through the wood-framed door and breathed a relieved sigh. Now a kitchen was a place she could feel comfortable in. "Thanks." She held out her hand, not caring why he knew she loved root beer nor that they were in the middle of an argument.

Holly would be fine as long as they arrived back at the time they'd left her. "You didn't answer me. Where are we? I'd say we were at Buckingham Palace, but something tells me I'd be wrong."

Ian leaned his ass against the stainless-steel counter and opened an ale. It was nothing like her best friend served in the pub back in Kentucky. It was probably some European brand.

He took a swig then focused on her. "This is my home, or rather my family's home. Make that a replica of my family's home since my father and mother still live in it when they are in Scotland though never at the same time."

"This is where you lived when you were alive?" This was more what she had originally envisioned heaven looking like, except maybe there'd be a pool with a few cabana boys at her beck and call.

"No. I had a flat in Glasgow."

She stared at him. "Oh, I can see why you'd prefer a little more space here."

"It was not a small flat. It was the entire top floor of Raven House on Garriochmill Road."

She had no clue what that meant, but a penthouse she'd seen on a television show about the wealthy gave her an idea. "So why don't you live there in the afterlife. I live in my apartment above the ice cream shop."

She took a sip of root beer, suddenly wishing she had vanilla ice cream to go with it.

Ian's face tightened. "Because I chose not to."

Didn't that just open up a whole can of worms? She definitely needed to do some digging on her partner. "Okay, so why did you bring me here? Yelling at me isn't going to sway me to your opinion." She held her root beer bottle up and moved it around in a circle. "And this rich living may impress me, but it's irrelevant to the point. Holly hasn't seen her family in two years. She's all alone, a widow, and needs her family."

"I agree."

She'd been about to take another sip when she stilled. "You agree?"

"Yes."

Oh boy, now he was back to one word answers. "Then we will take Holly to New Hampshire."

"No."

She finished her sip and put the bottle down on what looked like a butcher-block coffin. Who had cutting boards this big? Who could possibly make decent use of it? "You answered in the negative, which according to our agreement, you must explain."

He raised one eyebrow. "I didn't actually acquiesce to anything."

Great. Now he was bringing out the big words. If his goal was to impress her, it wasn't working. "Just tell me why you don't want Holly to visit her family tonight in her phased form when you just agreed that she deserves to see them."

He stood there and stared at her.

"Ian." She threw her hands up.

"You really don't like me, do you?"

Oh shoot, now she felt bad. "It's not a matter of liking or disliking. You're just irritating. In fact, I think you do it on purpose."

He blinked as if she'd figured him out. Oh, she was on to something here. "Yes, you make sure that no one wants to be around you."

His gaze left hers, confirming her suspicions. Ian Fergusson was an arrogant asshole on purpose to keep people from liking him. Her heart raced at the challenge her insight presented her. Before this case was over, she would discover why. "I'm sorry. I shouldn't have said that. Can we get back to Holly and your explanation of why you are so adamant that she *not* see her family?"

"Apology accepted." He took another swig of ale. "Holly *does* deserve to see her family, so why hasn't she? She's the only one who is keeping her from doing so. Have you noticed she uses the shop as a crutch?"

"I did notice that, but it *is* her livelihood."

Ian shook his head. "I'm sure there are slow weeks for a Christmas Shop such as hers. No, it's an excuse not to join the living, not to get involved, not to visit her family."

She took a deep breath. She agreed so far, but still couldn't fathom why he'd want to continue to deny her. "So we help her to do that. Let her see what she's missing. It might make her homesick enough to finally get on a plane."

"Or it might satisfy her that they are all okay and now that she's seen them, she doesn't have to go."

She picked up her root beer again. "But we agreed she *deserves* to see them."

"But not until she gets herself on a plane and does it herself. We need to keep her from seeing them to motivate her."

She took another sip pondering why his tactic bothered her so much. "Oh, you're punishing her. She's not a child."

He hesitated before answering. "I know it appears to be punishment, but I see it as incentive."

She shook her head. "What makes you think after two years she will suddenly fly home?"

His gray eyes turned crafty. "First, because you dangled the carrot in front of her. Right now, her anticipation is building. She can't wait to see her family again. If we return and tell her we decided against it, she will be very disappointed, so much so that after Hogmanay, she will probably get on a plane to America."

Great, now she looked like the bad guy. "And?"

His lips twitched and a tiny smile lifted their corners. "Second, we will be there to guide her, directing her thinking down the right avenue."

Ian Fergusson as an arrogant asshole was a hunk in every

way possible, but when he actually let himself smile, even a little, it transformed him. His gray eyes lightened and all the angles in his face softened. Seriously, he would be devastating.

That scared her. "You mean make her think what we want her to."

He shook his head, the slight lift to his lips remaining. "No, just nudge her a wee bit in the right direction."

Double shoot. Suddenly, she became aware of Ian's accent. Usually it wasn't as pronounced, but it was as if the softening of his features caused the lilt in his voice to become stronger.

She gulped down the rest of her root beer to avoid responding. That there was a human buried under the asshole shifted all her preconceptions of the man. He looked pleased and happy, not conniving like she'd expect. Oh, boy. "So if we deny Holly her visit with her family, what should be our next visit?"

Ian lost his smile and gave her a quick nod. "I promised you could choose the next one since I showed her Cameron's sister. What do you think?"

"I think she'll need to lift up her spirits. Maybe Brody's party or someone preparing for his party. That could be fun."

"I'm not sure if she's ready for that."

She swallowed her instinctive retort. Didn't he just agree she could choose? "Then how about Luca's family's party? She's not that close to him, so it would have less meaning but still might get her to long to celebrate as well."

He finished off his beer and threw the bottle in the trash though he didn't need to. It would disappear the instant they left the room. She'd fought hard to keep her place messy, even going to Mrs. Ferrisletter for help on how to make that happen. The afterlife had a ton of perks, but sometimes it wasn't perfect or maybe too perfect.

"No."

Ian's answer pulled her back on track. "No? You're saying no again. Why?"

He folded his arms over his wide chest, stretching the sleeves of his polo shirt to the max. He'd also crossed his legs. Talk about mixed messages. His body said *I'm relaxed and assured below,* but *uptight and closed off above.* She could probably make a study of the man for the rest of her afterlife and enjoy it…if he didn't irritate her so much. "So? A 'no' requires an explanation."

He raised that right eyebrow of his. "She's not ready for that."

She wasn't completely sure Holly was either or she'd tell him where he could go, but his track record was as good as hers. She sighed. "Very well, we take her to Sophia's sister. Do you think that will be depressing enough?" Yeah, she was pouting, but she didn't like the idea that he was *"nudging her a wee bit."*

He nodded, uncrossing his arms. "Yes."

Lovely, and they were back to one word answers again. Purposefully, she left her empty bottle on the butcher block and headed into the next room. At the sound of the bottle hitting the bottom of the trash can, she smiled. She was definitely going to loosen this man up.

She stopped in front of the fireplace with the angry man. "Who's that?"

His footsteps halted behind her. Without even looking, she could feel the tension increase in the room.

"My father." Ian's voice was flat. No emotion whatsoever in his tone.

She doubted the man in the painting was that controlled. She could easily see him yelling and making a young Ian feel like a piece of shit. Oh. Another puzzle piece fell into place. "Nothing personal—" she turned and looked at Ian. "But I don't like him."

Ian's face softened as if he might grace her with one of those little smiles, but it didn't happen. "I didn't like him much myself."

She frowned in puzzlement. "Then why do you have him here over the fireplace?"

He shrugged. "That's where the painting was when I was alive."

That still didn't make sense. At the ice cream shop she managed, where her apartment was upstairs, they never had enough Rocky Road to satisfy her, so in her afterlife place, one of the freezers was filled with it. They could have anything they wanted now. "This looks like a family home. You didn't stay in your flat in Glasgow when you transitioned?" No one said the "d" word here.

He came to stand next to her and stared at his father's portrait. "No."

She turned her head to give him a scowl, but he must have anticipated her response.

"I preferred to come home." The sneer on his face said it was the last place he wanted to be.

The man was too full of secrets. Was it his nature or was it pain that kept everything inside him? Oh.

Chapter Five

"Why are we going to see Sophia? I thought we were headed for my mom's house. That's like two opposite extremes." Holly frowned at them.

"I'll let Coco explain." Ian looked at her and her nose scrunched up in disgust before she smiled kindly at Holly. If he wasn't in their company, he would have chuckled. Coco's button nose when it moved like that was adorable.

"I really wanted you to see your family, but there are other places we need to bring you that you couldn't go to on your own, so we thought it a better use of our time here to let you fly home on your own."

Holly peered at him before shifting her gaze back to Coco. "You two agreed on this?"

He nodded, but Coco remained still.

Holly shook her head. "I don't buy it."

He frowned at her. "You don't buy what?"

"You two can take us through time, any time on Christmas Eve, which means we have all the time in the world."

"That's not exactly true." Coco may think he treated Holly like a child, but he wouldn't do that. "We are limited in our time with you and you are perfectly capable of getting on a plane and visiting your family. However, you are not capable of visiting Sophia's sister."

Holly's chin came down at that. "Sophia has a sister?"

He raised his eyebrow, but didn't say anymore. This was Coco's visit. She should take the lead.

Coco threw up her hands. "Don't try to get any more out of him. When he stops talking, there's no getting him to start up again. Why don't you take our hands so we can make our next stop?"

"So we really can't see my family?" Holly's face was pure heartbreak. Even he had to steel himself against acquiescing.

Coco never broke eye contact with Holly. "No, I'm afraid not. Why haven't you gone before now?"

"I told you, I have the shop."

Coco didn't respond.

Ian watched, fascinated. His partner didn't look menacing or stern. In fact, a sympathetic smile played about her mouth. She *was* good.

Holly crossed her arms. "Okay. Maybe I can look into flights after Hogmanay. I really do miss them."

"That sounds like a great idea." Coco's smile widened.

He could get lost in that smile. It was fast becoming his greatest wish and his greatest fear.

Holly nodded. "Well, you do have me curious." She glanced at him. "I'm ready."

At first, he wasn't sure what she meant, but then he redirected his thoughts back to their current task and grasped Holly's hand. Coco took her other and they flew high into the sky, heading northeast.

"I love this flying part." Holly beamed at him then looked away toward Coco.

Coco spoiled the moment, most likely on purpose. "This will be a short trip." Even as she said it, they floated down through the roof of the Erskine Cancer Center near Glasgow.

They stopped in a hallway in the north wing. Holly looked

around but she didn't say anything as Coco led them to the door of a room halfway down the hall. There were no decorations on the walls and the sterile atmosphere was stifling.

In retrospect, he was glad that Ella never had to experience it.

The hospital room door opened and Sophia stepped out. Before the door closed, she leaned in. "Are you sure you don't want chocolate?"

A voice inside answered, and Sophia closed the door. She walked toward them. There was nothing confident or pompous about her now.

Holly pulled her hands from their grasp to watch Sophia enter an elevator. When the woman turned around to push the button, they all saw the tears falling on her cheeks.

"What's going on here?" Holly spun around and looked at him, but he nodded to Coco.

"Well?" She turned her attention to his partner.

"Sophia's younger sister has leukemia. She was in remission for a long time, but it has returned."

"Holy crap. That's awful. And it's Christmas Eve."

"I know." Coco turned away from the elevator. "It has to be hard on Sophia."

Holly hesitated before she finally spoke. "I never really liked Sophia because she is so self-involved, but I had no idea this was happening. Is it just me or is everyone clueless about this in Deervale?"

He answered. "No one is aware that Sophia has a sister with cancer."

"I don't understand." Holly looked back to Coco for edification.

"Why don't we go inside so we can learn some more?" Coco glanced at him and he nodded.

Just then the elevator doors opened and Sophia strode down the hall, no tears were evident anymore and she held a cup of strawberry ice cream. They followed her into the room.

The room was as festive as the hallway was not. He had to think even Holly would be impressed with how the Dunlaps had transformed the room.

A full sized artificial Christmas tree graced the corner, completely decorated and with a blinking star on top. Presents filled the floor beneath the tree and there was a Christmas rug next to the hospital bed. Even the window had evergreen bunting, and a small sprig of mistletoe hung strategically over the pillow, giving every visitor an excuse to kiss the patient.

"Here you go, wee sis. Strawberry like you wanted." Sophia shook her head as if she couldn't imagine anyone wanting anything but chocolate.

A teenage girl of sixteen sat cross-legged on the bed, her bald scalp partially covered with a wool ear warmer. She took the ice cream. "Thanks. You're the best sister. I can't believe you were able to talk mom and dad into going home tonight. They were driving me crazy."

Sophia laughed. "I figured you could use a break."

"You didn't get any for yourself?" The girl took a big bite of ice cream and licked her lips. "It's really good."

"Thea, eat that slowly. You know it's going to give you a stomach ache."

The teenager shrugged. "So I might as well enjoy it."

Ian watched Holly study Sophia. Did she see the dark circles under the woman's eyes or the worry lines in her brow? He hoped so.

"Don't you have a party to go to or something?" Thea pointed toward the dark window with her spoon.

"After the week I had shopping for all your presents? I'd much rather sit with you and relax than listen to local gossip about who is getting what for Christmas and who is planning what for Hogmanay."

Thea looked at the tree in the corner. "I love the angel ornament. It's perfect."

Sophia glanced at the ornament she'd bought earlier that day.

Holly floated over to it. "She said she bought it for herself. Why is she hiding this? I could help her."

Coco wrapped her arm around Holly's shoulder and floated her out of the room. "You can't tell her you know."

"Why not?"

"Think about it. How would she react if you said, 'Oh, Sophia, I'm so sorry about your sister. Is there anything I can do to help?' Would her answer be to ask you to make a special lunch or come with her to visit?"

Holly opened her mouth then closed it. She sighed. "No. She'd get defensive and want to know how I knew."

Coco simply nodded but Ian broke in. "She wouldn't trust you to keep the secret. Actually, she might think you heard it from someone else. That could cause her to leave Deervale all together."

"But why does she hide it? Why does she let everyone think she is so self-involved?"

Coco floated to a chair in the waiting room they had drifted toward when they exited the room. "Sophia *is* self-involved. That's not an act. Her parents doted on her as the oldest until Thea came along. Sophia loved her sister so she didn't mind sharing her parents' love, but when her sister came down with leukemia at the age of ten, everything changed in the Dunlap household."

Ian remained standing, but Holly floated into a chair opposite of Coco. "What happened?"

"What needed to happen. The parents focused on Thea and so did Sophia, but Sophia was only fifteen herself."

"And that's when we are so insecure. I know I was." Holly shook her head. "I was lucky my mom remarried us into the Tinders' family. After our apartment fire, I think I appreciated the love and support of them more than most teenagers would."

Coco cocked her head. "Can you imagine what it would be like to have all that attention switched to a sibling and know that you couldn't even rightfully resent it?"

"So that's why Sophia became focused on herself. No one else was. I guess that should teach me not to judge a book by its cover. Wait a minute, so why does Sophia live in Deervale when her sister is so sick. I'd think she'd want to be closer."

Coco shrugged. "Thea hasn't been sick these last five years. She was in remission for three. Now they are finishing her chemotherapy so they can try a bone marrow transplant."

Holly's eyes widened. "I really wish there was something I could do."

Ian shook his head. "You are always kind in action. I think simply with your new understanding of what has influenced Sophia's character, it will make it easier for you to continue to be."

"Is this why Cameron wanted me to see Thea? To help me be kind to her sister?"

Ian glanced at Coco. She caught his look and rose. "That was part of it."

Holly floated out of the chair and closer to Coco. "Tell me."

"He wanted you to see how some people have no choice but to celebrate Christmas in a hospital yet they are still with the ones they love."

Holly swallowed. "It's just hard for me. I feel like I'll bring everyone down if I join them for the holiday. You know, I am 'poor widow Douglas' in town."

Ian couldn't resist stepping in. "But they wouldn't call you that if you were out and about more, would they?"

Holly's face fell and Coco glared at him. She mouthed the words "she's not a child," before wrapping her arm around Holly. "I know you loved Cameron very much. You two were soulmates. It's hard to move on after a soulmate dies."

"You make it sound like what we had was extra special. That's how I felt." Holly looked at him. "Like we were meant to be together and then he died on me." Her anger triggered a response in him that he refused to acknowledge.

Coco pulled Holly into a full hug. "I'll tell you a secret, but you have to keep it to yourself. Only Cameron knows."

Holly's face lit with anticipation.

Her quick rebound in emotions gave Ian hope that they could help her as Cameron wished. Too bad his own heart couldn't adjust as easily.

"I promise." Holly crossed her chest. "I'm good with secrets."

Coco smiled. "I have always had the ability to recognize soulmates."

He barely kept himself from rolling his eyes.

"That's nice." Holly smiled politely.

"No, I don't think you understand. I can actually tell. For instance, you have a silver glow around you. That tells me you were in love with your soulmate but now he has moved on. When I see two people in the same area that are soulmates, I see matching golden glows around them. Sort of like an aura but much brighter and distinct, at least to me."

She could see soulmates? Is that why Cameron wanted her on this case? For the second time, he cursed the lack of information in Holly's file. Ian's gut told him that Cameron was up to more than what he'd revealed to them.

"So Cam and I really were supposed to find each other." Holly's eyes started to water.

Coco nodded. "And you will again. That's the good news."

Holly's gaze turned shrewd. "Did you find your soulmate? I mean, when you were alive?"

Coco turned to him. "No. I didn't." She smiled at Holly then, but it was forced and Ian's heart jerked.

"I knew in my gut that some man from another country was

destined to be my soulmate, but I never left Kentucky, so we didn't meet." Her face lit then. "But the people there that were soulmates were so many."

"Did you help them find each other?" Holly's question mirrored Ian's own. He had no knowledge of Coco's gift and now his curiosity was piqued. Could she tell if he had a silver glow? Was Ella his soulmate and he squandered their chance at real love?"

Coco lowered her voice as if they could be heard. It was a habit he found endearing. "I didn't point them out to each other, if that's what you mean. But if they asked, and many asked after they figured out I had a gift, I would tell them." She shrugged. "I didn't think it was my place to interfere."

"But it *is* a gift." Holly crossed her arms. "I would think you were meant to use it."

"Oh, I did. I just waited to be asked, except for once."

Holly's brown eyes sparkled with curiosity. "Once?"

Coco laughed. "We are not spending the night talking about me. This is your Christmas Eve and I'm sure Ian has something fittingly depressing planned for our next trip."

Both women looked to him and it took all he had not to respond to their smiles with one of his own. He shouldn't feel this good. It wasn't appropriate. He raised his eyebrow. "As a matter of fact, I thought we should visit young Luca, who as a teenager, knows how to celebrate the holiday in style."

Coco's pretty mouth fell open and Holly laughed. "Sounds good to me."

He ignored the glare coming from his partner and inserted himself between the two. Taking each one in hand, he flew them back to Deervale.

Coco gritted her teeth. The urge to yell at the man holding her hand was that strong. First, he convinced her that Holly wasn't ready for holiday cheer, making her bring her on a difficult visit and the next thing she knows, he's bringing Holly to a party! They were so going to have a talk after this stunt.

The three of them landed in the banquet hall of the Loudon Hill Tavern and Guest Cottages. One corner of the room was set up with couches and easy chairs where many older folks were lounging, a drink from the bar in the next room in their hands.

Banquet tables lined one wall and were filled with truffles, shortbreads, a few clootie dumplings and other treats, as well as various punches and fizzy juice. The room was decked out in pine bunting, Christmas decorations and a Christmas tree.

Ian settled them down at the opposite end of the room where the teenagers huddled in packs not far from the band, which was settling into their places. Coco immediately withdrew her hand from Ian's. He raised that eyebrow of his at her move but didn't say anything. She was positive he knew exactly what he'd done.

Holly pointed. "There's Luca. He bought a lovely ornament for his new girlfriend. I'm guessing the blonde standing next to him will be the happy recipient. He said she was into netball and she looks pretty athletic." Holly looked up at Ian, who once again hovered just a little higher than them.

"Last year it was a glass ballet dancer for what he termed a girlie." She moved her gaze to Coco. "I think that means she was a 'girly girl', as we'd say in America."

Coco nodded to show she understood, but as soon as Holly turned back to watch Luca, she floated away toward the food tables. She wasn't sure she wanted to be a part of this particular visit. She'd been manipulated and it pissed her off. And when she was mad, she ate, so looking at the treats might help calm her down.

She'd just done a complete scan of all the delectables when the band started playing. It was older music obviously intended to get the adults out on the floor. It didn't take long for them to accept the invitation either.

Coco hovered over what looked to be a fruit tart of some kind. She could use a piece of that right about now.

Ian's voice floated over the crowd to her just like he floated above them all the time. "I believe more than one of your ornaments will be gifted tonight."

"How do you know?" Holly's excitement at that prospect had Coco looking at them.

Ian waved his hand over the presents beneath the Christmas tree. The contents of each box was revealed. At least half the gifts were from the One of a Kind Christmas Shop.

Ian placed his hand on Holly's shoulder. "Do you see how important you are to this community? Imagine the joy these will bring to the receivers of these gifts."

Coco balled her hands into fists. He wasn't supposed to reveal the inside of presents. What was he doing? She flew back across the room. "Ian, we need to talk."

"We do?"

"Yes. What you just did. You can't do that."

He frowned, his face taking on the hard lines she always associated with him. "There is no rule requiring me to refrain from showing Holly that the shop she created with Cameron is an important part of life in Deervale."

She clamped down hard on a retort. The man was too fricking good at couching his actions in terms of their client. Technically, they could do anything to help Holly rejoin the living, but Ian walked a tightrope with his revelations. If he fell, she wasn't sure she wanted to catch him.

Even at that thought, she chastised herself. Now who wasn't being nice? She tried to find middle ground. "I'm sure Holly already knows how important she has become to Deervale."

She looked at Cameron's wife. "Do you feel like part of this community?"

Holly nodded. "I do. I think that's why I haven't flown home to see my family. I know they will want me to move back to America and I can't. This is where Cam is. Was."

Ian's frown grew colder, but Coco ignored him. "I can understand that. But to these people, you are not simply Cameron Douglas' wife. You are Holly, the smiling lady at the Christmas shop, who finds the perfect items for them to show the most important people in their lives just how much they are loved."

"Ahem." Ian's reminder that this was his visit was loud and clear.

She looked at him, her smile completely fake. "Just lending a hand."

When his scowl deepened, she floated to the other side of Holly, not completely sorry she'd interrupted his little lecture. She wasn't happy being manipulated, and they were going to have a heart to heart before the next visit.

She finally relaxed and studied the occupants of the room. Her heart warmed to see almost half the adult and older adult couples who were dancing were glowing. There was something about watching soulmates together that filled her with happiness and just a tinge of wistfulness.

It was then she noticed the boy, Luca. He had a golden glow as well. That meant his soulmate was in the room and it wasn't the young woman he was talking to. Coco floated higher to see better above the crowd, her heart picking up speed at identifying a soulmate. It never got old, not even in the afterlife.

A pretty brunette who laughed with her friends near the cookie tray glowed as well. Coco floated over to listen to the girls' conversation, but after a few minutes, it was clear that Luca was not a topic. If she were alive, she'd find a way for them to meet. The rest would be up to them.

She glanced back toward Ian to find him staring at her, that one eyebrow raised.

Oh, what the frick, finding soulmates was just too exciting not to share. Flying over the crowd, she was almost to him and Holly when a light caught her attention to her right. She stopped and stared.

There was a young lady bringing her grandmother a pretty plaid shawl. It wasn't the shawl that caught her attention, but the glow emanating from the teenager. Coco rose higher to have all three young people in her sight. Oh, wow!

She spun and flew to Holly and Ian. "You're not going to believe this, but Luca has two soulmates right here in this room! That's almost unheard of. The same town is rare as it is, but the same room?"

Holly's eyes rounded with excitement. "Really? A person can have two soulmates?"

Coco grinned. Happiness filled her and there was no containing it. "Yes. I have no idea how many we can have but I know it's more than one as I've seen this before, but never in the same room. It's amazing! Can you feel it?"

Holly nodded. "You have to tell me who. Is one of them the girl Luca bought the ornament for?"

She shook her head. "Nope. Neither of his soulmates appears to know he exists. If I was alive, I would arrange to have them meet without saying anything." She gazed at Holly's happy face. "It always brought me pleasure to make the connection possible, but I never interfered. I didn't think that would be right." Actually, she had once, but she wasn't going to explain the extenuating circumstances. "As humans, we have free will to make our own choices."

"Well, you could tell me and I could try and arrange for them to at least meet." Holly looked so hopeful.

There was no rule for this specific instance and she found

herself glancing toward Ian. He nodded his agreement. For some reason that made her feel a lot safer about telling Holly. The rules in the afterlife were few, but the consequences of breaking them were fatal.

She pointed. "See the young lady with her friends walking towards the band? The one with the white top and green plaid skirt?"

Holly nodded. "I think she's a little more interested in one of the musicians than Luca at the moment."

Coco agreed. "The other is over there, next to that older woman in the wheel chair. The one with the black curly hair."

Holly scanned the crowd before locating the teenager. "Oh look, I think she's spotted Luca."

She wanted to hug Holly in glee. To share this experience with someone else again was pure happiness for her. "Do you know who she is?"

"No, but maybe I can figure it out by listening to her conversation with the older woman."

Coco laughed, too happy to hold it in. "Great idea." She floated them over to listen.

Ian's hand on her shoulder startled her and she spun around to face him, but not before he whisked them outside the hall onto the cold, quiet hill nearby.

She blinked at the change in scenery. Loudon Hill was dark and empty of any holiday warmth. It was like a bucket of ice being thrown on her emotions. She glared at Ian. "What?"

"This is not about you."

She stared at him, speechless. His gray eyes in the limited moonlight were hard steel and his face could have been chiseled from Cairngorm crystal. She was well aware of why he'd ticked her off, but what had she done? He agreed she could show Holly who Luca's soulmates were, so what the frick? "I think I'm experienced enough to know that my job is not about me."

His face didn't change an iota. "From what I saw in there, it was all about you."

She slammed her hands on her hips. "Seriously? Holly was excited to learn that a person could have more than one soulmate. Not only that, *she* wanted to help Luca find his. What has that got to do with me?"

He turned away from her and crossed his arms, but he didn't say a word.

Oh no, he was not going to accuse her of something and not explain himself. She floated around him and high enough to face him eye to eye. "There's nothing wrong with finding a little joy in our assignments. Exciting events call for laughter, something it's hard to imagine you doing. I'm certainly not turning into a stone for you."

Ian pushed right through her and strode across the barren hill top.

"Now what has gotten into you?" She flew after him. "I'm the one who should be pissed. You manipulated me into bringing Holly to see heartbreak while you invite her to a party."

He stopped so suddenly, she flew a few feet ahead before realizing he was behind her. She turned back to face him.

"This is not about fun and games. We need to instruct Holly in the lessons she needs to join the living. *That* is our assignment. It's not about how she views either of us. Again, you are focused on yourself."

She frowned, her own self-doubt making her question if he was right. No. He was manipulating her again. She shook her head. "Is this how you were in life? Manipulative? Getting people to do what you wanted, how you wanted it?"

Ian's eyes widened. "You don't know anything about my life."

She floated back a foot at the hard rage in his eyes. Boy, did she step in the shit patch or what? She didn't know anything about his life, but it was time she found out. "So tell me."

"Tell you?" His voice was barely above a growl.

"Yes. Tell me about your life."

This time he did growl, a sound filled with anger, frustration, and loathing. "No."

"If you won't—"

Ian vanished.

"Great."

Chapter Six

The rage burned, making him want to throw himself against a wall, but it would do no good. He would still exist, still feel, still know he'd failed.

He sped through time and space, heedless of where he went. His father's words ringing in his ears. *You couldn't even love someone the right way. You're worthless.*

None of it mattered since he could be anywhere he wanted any time with no one else to hurt. If only life could have been that way.

Instead, he'd hurt everyone. His father. His family. His fiancée. He stopped, suddenly aware he was back in his Glasgow flat, the scene of the crime.

He didn't dare move. He floated in his living room, where he hadn't been since he started as a spirit guide.

He didn't want to be here.

Slowly, he turned toward the hall to the bedroom. Ella would be there. Deceptively peaceful in her final sleep, the empty bottle of pills lying on the carpeted floor. Their argument of the night before like a cast iron weight tied around his neck.

You tell me you love me, but you don't mean it. You're not with me, not really. I need your heart, Ian, not your words.

I am here, Ella. You make me whole.

No. You're already whole. I'm the one with missing pieces, pieces you don't need.

Please Ella, it's just the stress of the wedding. You know we're meant to be together. Please don't shake your head. It kills me inside when you push me away.

Maybe I need too much. More than you can give me.

"Ian?"

He started at the new voice in his head. Who?

"Ian, what happened here?"

Coco. She'd found him.

He looked at the now empty bed, his dead fiancée gone. It was his due punishment.

In a daze of pain, he moved his gaze to Coco. Warm, happy, full of life, full of curves. He wanted her even while standing where his fiancée had taken her own life. He wanted all that she was and he wasn't.

Her hand on his arm made him shudder, the sudden warmth like heat to a cold glass. He jerked away from her. "You followed me." His mouth felt like it was filled with sawdust as he formed the words.

"I did. I was worried. You vanished in the middle of our conversation." Her brow wrinkled with concern. "You know the last two spirits assigned to Holly's case never came back. You scared me."

It'd be better off for everyone if he did disappear, for all their sakes. But here he remained, to be punished for being "emotionally unobtainable." *Thanks, Father.*

"Do you want to talk about it?" Coco's golden eyes were filled with sympathy, honest feeling.

He shook his head, his equilibrium slowly returning. "No." His loss of control solidified for him his need to work alone. It had been her pure joy shared with Holly over soulmates that had infuriated him, caused him to lose control. He wouldn't let it happen again.

She raised one eyebrow and smiled at him in expectation of an explanation.

"Are you imitating me? Because if you are, you are failing miserably."

She shrugged. "It was worth a shot."

"I suggest we get back to our assignment." He opened his arm to allow her to proceed him, but she stayed where she was and cocked her head.

"Not so fast. What was that all about?" She waved her hand around in a circle as if it made "that" more clear.

He was quite aware of what she referred to, but had no plans to address it. "I apologize for my behavior."

"You do? Okay, that's good." She nodded her head as if she had to make herself believe he had apologized.

"Where would you like to take Holly next?" Anxious to leave his flat, he hoped she'd take the bait and be distracted from him.

"Are you really going to allow me to decide?"

He nodded once. "Your choice. I'll base my next visit on Holly's reaction to yours."

"Hmmm." She studied him. "I'm not sure I entirely trust you after you manipulated me so beautifully last time."

He kept silent. He had done exactly that. Another bad habit he'd inherited from his father.

She floated to the window that looked out onto the stone bridge by his flat.

He may be a spirit, but he was also a man. The swirl of Coco's skirts had him watching her pass by and he was not immune to the view he had of her substantial cleavage in the square neckline of her Christmas dress, just one advantage to floating higher than she.

That he was physically attracted to her in addition to craving her warmth just increased his self-disgust. She should stay as far from him as possible.

"Mrs. Bell's." She spun around and faced him. "I want to take her to Mrs. Bell's house."

"A good choice."

She frowned. "Shoot. Then maybe I should choose somewhere else."

"Whatever you like." He kept any emotion from showing, but he kicked himself for making her doubt her instincts.

"Boy, you make this difficult." She flounced over to him. "You know that, right?"

Yes, he knew. "I did not intend for it to be so."

"Hmm, I guess I'll have to take your word for it." She held out her hand. "Let's go."

He entwined his fingers with hers, anxious to move on and get the assignment finished, but as they flew through the ether, he couldn't help wondering if there would be an actual end or if they too would disappear.

At that thought, he squeezed her hand tighter. Whatever happened to him, he didn't want to take Coco with him.

If Ian Fergusson thought for one second that she'd forgotten what he'd done, he was sorely mistaken. She'd play along, pretend to be focused on Holly, but she was bound and determined to discover what made the man tick.

Something terrible had happened at that flat. Something that gnawed on him as if he were a bone for a dog. Maybe if she could help him get over whatever it was, he would be allowed to move up to adult assignments.

She was surprised she felt that way, after all, he was the arrogant asshole, but just like Sophia, something had occurred in his life to make him the way he was. She grimaced. She had no doubt that father of his had something to do with it.

But now that she'd discovered the man was somewhat human,

she was determined to help him. He could do so much good among the living if he could come to terms with whatever happened in his flat. If she was honest with herself, she wanted him to be human. A man with so much intelligence shouldn't go to waste. Plus, there was that awesome body of his. She grinned.

Who knew? Maybe there was also a chance helping him would solidify her chances of gaining a position as spirit guide trainer. It hadn't been a goal of hers, but now that Mrs. Ferrisletter had suggested it, she really liked the idea.

They met up with Holly, who quickly discovered the names of both soulmates for Luca. Then they moved on to Mrs. Bell's home. As soon as they phased through the front door, they could hear her talking.

"I wonder if Mrs. Bell has company?" Coco led the way past a never used parlor, into a dining room with a table filled with boxes. Finally, they found her in the kitchen. She had a red apron on with green holly leaves sewn on the bib. It covered a pretty light blue floral dress that accented Mrs. Bell's pristine white hair.

"Oh look." Holly pointed to a chair at the small kitchen table piled with dirty baking bowls, spoons and utensils. "A ghost."

It *was* a ghost and a female one at that.

Ian drifted closer to the ghost. "It's Mrs. Bell's older sister. She passed over a decade before now." He looked at Holly. "You've seen ghosts before?"

Holly nodded solemnly. "Yes. Scary ones at the bottom of Louden Hill and mischievous ones in northern New Hampshire. And then Jessica almost turned into one."

"What?" Coco stared at Holly. "You mean Jessica the Spirit of Christmas Past?"

Holly nodded. "Yes. Last I saw her, she was fading into a ghost, but Duncan said he could help her."

Coco swallowed hard. Becoming a ghost meant a person's soul

was trapped with the living forever, which completely rattled her. "How could she become a ghost if she didn't have any unfinished business. If that was true, she would have never become a spirit to begin with."

Ian's hand on her shoulder helped her take deeper breaths. She was panicking, but the idea that one of them could turn into a ghost had never crossed her mind and it scared the frick out of her.

Holly frowned. "I asked Cameron if she was okay after she and Duncan left, and he said she was great."

Coco looked back at Ian, who floated behind her. How could Jessica be great if she was no longer with them? Cameron hid something important from everyone.

Ian squeezed her shoulder and nodded toward Holly. Of course, she needed to focus.

It was just a bit too close to home for her. She technically had unfinished business in that she'd never met her soulmate, but she always thought that was different because it wasn't as if she'd met him and lost him.

But then wouldn't that make Cameron a ghost instead of a spirit because he was so attached to Holly? Shoot. Maybe she needed to get a few more clarifications from Mrs. Ferrisletter.

"Meg, do you think these mince pies are overdone? I do think I may have cooked them too long." Mrs. Bell spoke to her sister as if she could hear, and it appeared she could. The ghost shook her head.

"Maybe I best put one more batch in just to be sure I have enough." Mrs. Bell glanced at the clock on the wall. "Then I must figure out what to wear. Can you believe that lovely Sarah Gowan and her fiancé invited me to their Christmas Eve party? I probably should have said I couldn't go because I still have so much baking to do, but really, it is Christmas Eve after all. Everyone should take some time to celebrate."

Meg, the ghost, nodded in agreement.

Coco stared hard at Holly until the woman flushed and looked away. One message sent and delivered.

The three of them watched as Mrs. Bell filled another tray with mince pies and put them in the oven.

The older woman continued to talk to her sister as if it was habit. "There, now I just need to pack up Mr. Wrenford's desserts to go with the dinner I made for him and I can start getting ready. Oh, Meg, I do wish you could come with me. I so miss our Christmases together."

The ghost smiled sadly as Mrs. Bell went into the next room to pick out a box.

Holly floated to the dessert waiting to be packaged. "I'm so glad I asked Brody to invite Mrs. Bell. Just look at all this. I think she lives in her kitchen."

Coco had to agree. "I doubt her parlor has been used in decades. Did you see the dust on the side tables?"

Holly looked to Ian. "You said Mrs. Bell's sister died over a decade ago. That was before I married Cameron. Did the sisters live together?"

"Yes, they did." He floated back toward Meg. "She doted on her little sister and moved in with her shortly after Mr. Bell died. They were only married a few years before he was killed in combat. Meg never married."

At the mention of her name, the ghost looked at Ian.

Coco caught her breath. "I think she can hear us."

Ian stared right at the ghost. "Meg, can you hear me?"

The woman nodded and spoke, but they couldn't hear *her*.

Ian shook his head and lifted his hands.

Meg immediately understood and rose from her chair to pantomime a message. Holly guessed, but Ian had to say the words in order for Meg to hear them. It must be his tone of voice or...Coco stilled. Maybe he was closer to being a ghost than he should be?

Holly laughed excitedly. "She wants us to get Mr. Wrenford and Mrs. Bell together."

Ian repeated the words and Meg nodded as she floated back into her seat.

Mrs. Bell took that moment to come in with a pretty red and green plaid box. As she lined it with colored tissue paper followed by parchment paper, her older sister pointed. It was the box for Mr. Wrenford.

"I have an idea." Holly grasped Coco's arm. "Can we go to Mr. Wrenford's right now?"

She looked at Ian. "I'm fine with that."

He addressed Holly. "Why do you want to go to his house now?"

Holly's eyes were alight with mischief. "I'm curious about him. Except for the fact that he eats out every meal that isn't prepared by Mrs. Bell, I don't know that much about him. Since he's never come to my shop, I'm guessing he has no one to buy Christmas presents for."

Coco took Holly's hand. "He could simply shop online and have them sent, you know."

Holly laughed. "I don't think so."

Ian didn't say anything, but she knew he was behind them as they flew down a couple streets to Main Street then toward the opposite end from Holly's home.

Coco still wanted to discover what had happened to Ian in his past that would set him off on her at Luca's party, but for now she was happy he'd regained his composure.

They entered Mr. Wrenford's home through the front door, like they had at Mrs. Bell's. Coco preferred that over roof top entrances. Those seemed too intrusive.

Mr. Wrenford sat at his dining room table. The telly was on but he wasn't paying any attention to it. He was busy playing cards.

There was a three-foot Christmas tree on a table in the parlor, but it wasn't lit.

"Bah, stupid king." He added another card to a pile and picked up three more. He continued to play his game in silence.

None of them spoke, the scene a little sad. Coco moved back into the parlor. She found three Christmas cards set on the mantel, but the electric fireplace was cold.

Holly found her. "Can you make me solid, so I can knock on his door?"

Of any request, Coco had never expected that one. "Why?"

"I want to tell him that Brody has asked him to pick up Mrs. Bell and bring her to the party." Holly beamed, very proud of her matchmaking idea.

"I'm sorry. I can't do that."

Holly's face fell. "Why not?"

"Yes, why not?" Ian floated into the room. "It's the perfect solution for Mr. Wrenford, who has nothing else to do tonight. Also for Mrs. Bell, who won't have to walk to the party in the cold with all her boxes. And for Meg."

She looked at him as if he'd told her he wanted to go Easter egg hunting. "Excuse me? Because we are supposed to phase our client and bring her into places she couldn't otherwise see, or could see if she actually decided to leave her house." She glanced at Holly who caught her message.

"Holly could have walked or driven to Mr. Wrenford's easily tonight, so why not make her solid?" Ian's brow was drawn down in puzzlement.

At least he didn't have his eyebrow raised. She was tiring of that.

It had never been done. Was this one of those lines if they crossed they'd never return? Ian may not feel he had anything to lose, but she liked her afterlife. "Have you ever done this before?"

He shrugged. "That's hardly relevant. The fact is, we are in the present, so any actions on Holly's part do not change the past. I see no harm."

"No harm? But this would be changing the future, not only because we brought her here, but also because she was privy to Mrs. Bell's dead sister's wishes! Holly would not have walked over here and started this if we were not involved."

Coco was well aware that Holly watched them both, one minute smiling and the next not. Coco didn't want to disappoint her, but there could be greater ramifications, not just for Holly and Mrs. Bell, but for her and Ian.

"The future is always changing." Ian shrugged. "Every time Cameron or one of the other supervisors sends spirits to the living, we are changing the future. That, if I'm not mistaken, is the whole point." He paused.

At least he gave their argument the weight it deserved.

He continued, "As spirits of Christmas Present, we have the option then to solidify Holly, something Spirits of the Past couldn't do."

Coco put her hands on her hips. "Yes, but Spirits of the Future can't either or they would change the past. We are all connected. You can't simply let her change the present. What makes you think we have a right no other spirit does?"

Ian grabbed Holly's hand and brought her outside.

Coco grabbed his arm. "Don't do it."

He stared down his nose at her, his irritation clear in his eyes. "No one has said it can't be done. There's no rule you can point to, no punishment you can cite that forbids solidifying a client in the present. So…"

"Wait!" Holly pulled her hand from his. "If I show up in my bathrobe, he'll wonder what's wrong with me. I can just hear him now, grumbling about the crazy American widow."

Coco grinned and crossed her arms. "So great Spirit of Christmas Present, what are you going to do about that?"

Ian actually looked uncomfortable.

"I know." Holly gave her puppy dog eyes. "We can go back to my place, unphase me so I can dress then phase me again and bring me back here at this time."

Coco couldn't help it. She raised her right eyebrow at Ian. It was no small feat. Her eyebrows didn't like working separately of each other. Ian knew they couldn't go back in present time once they started the night.

He frowned at both she and Holly, his gaze moving between them. Suddenly, he grinned. Not a quirk of the lips, but an actual small smile. It was a triumphant, "I'm brilliant" smile, but it didn't matter. That smile softened his features and made her wish she could kiss him.

Holy frick, where did that come from?

"You two can change." Ian's gaze traveled over her body, heating her from her face to her feet. "You look about the same size."

She shook her head. "I don't think so."

"Please, Coco. Just for a few minutes." Holly's round dark eyes were hard to resist, but she continued to shake her head.

"For me then, lass?" Ian's deep voice was soft, his eyes seductive and his mouth still in that smile that weakened her knees and made it hard to breathe.

She took a deep breath and started to shake her head when Ian caught her chin in his hand. He turned her toward him and lowered his face closer to hers. "Please dinna say nay to this poor man. There ina much that I find pleasure in anymore."

Oh, boy. She couldn't resist the heavy accent on top of the unguarded look of desire in his eyes. His gray gaze had grown dark and his spruce scent filled the air around her, flooding her senses.

She wasn't made of stone. She nodded.

Instead of pulling away now that he'd gotten his way, Ian's mouth lowered.

She closed her eyes at the touch of his lips on hers. Every nerve in her body, every blood vessel, focused on the brush of his kiss. It was gentle, barely a touch, just enough for her to want more.

She opened her eyes as his hand left her chin, and he floated backward. Now he would be impossible to deal with, convinced he could get his way whenever he wanted. What had she been thinking?

But as she looked at him, his own gaze was elsewhere and a frown furrowed his brow. At least he didn't gloat. She had expected that.

"So can we change now?" Holly's voice snapped her back to the issue.

Frick, she'd actually caved all because of a stupid smile and a little charm, but she had no choice now. "Yes, let's go around the corner and switch."

She led the way to the back of Mr. Wrenford's house and they quickly changed. Holly's robe was a little snug, but Coco tied the belt tight. Her own dress was a tad large for Holly, but Mr. Wrenford would never notice in the dark of night.

When they were done, they floated back to where Ian stood.

"Are you ready?" Ian scanned Holly's attire. "Be sure your feet touch the ground."

Holly lowered herself another half foot before Ian unphased her. With a brilliant smile, she walked up the steps to Mr. Wrenford's house and knocked.

They could hear his chair slide back on the floor and his footsteps as he drew closer.

Coco leaned into Ian, ignoring his sharp scent this time, and whispered. "I hope you know what you're doing."

He gazed down at her. "I have no idea."

What? She opened her mouth to give him a piece of her mind when Mr. Wrenford greeted Holly. Snapping her mouth shut, she remained silent while Holly asked the man to bring Mrs. Bell.

He looked behind Holly. "You can't bring her yourself?"

Holly smiled. "If I had driven I would have, but I was on my way to another friend's house when Brody called. Surely you don't mind. I mean, after all the food Mrs. Bell has cooked for you. I wouldn't be surprised if she has something special for you for Christmas as well."

The old man's interest was caught with that. "I guess it is the neighborly thing to do. When did you say I need to get her there?"

While the two living people discussed the particulars, Coco turned to Ian. He wasn't watching Holly. Instead, his gaze was further down the main street where two people walked arm and arm. She couldn't tell who it was.

Studying his profile, she could see the strain in his features, his jaw was tight and his neck muscles taut. She glanced at the couple strolling closer. They were obviously in love and very happy, but Ian looked as if he hated them. No, resented them.

"Ian?" She kept her voice to a whisper, almost afraid to interrupt his thoughts.

He snapped his head around and in the brief moment before he recalled where he was, she saw it. Harsh pain and self-loathing so strong that she involuntarily floated back.

The man was tortured. She'd never seen a spirit in so much pain. They needed to get to the bottom of it. Cameron's words echoed in her mind. *He's the only one who can get the job done and it's as important to him as it is to me, though he doesn't know it yet.*

Instinct told her Ian was with her on this assignment so she could help him, too.

His gaze had returned to the usual bored, slightly superior look he generally wore. "Yes?"

They couldn't leave Holly while she was solid, so Coco skipped to the other topic on her mind. "Have you decided where you would like to take Holly next?"

"I have."

He turned his face to watch Holly say goodbye to Mr. Wrenford. He really could be an arrogant asshole when he wanted to be, but she wasn't fooled anymore. "And where would that be?"

"It worked!" Holly walked to the end of the sidewalk, her ability to see them only possible thanks to Cameron's preparations. "You can phase me again."

Ian laid his hand on her shoulder and she phased. "Coco, this is the most awesome holiday dress. Whose tartan is it?"

Ian floated a bit higher. "It's mine."

Holly's gaze flew to her. "Really?"

"Yes. I'm not Scottish, so I picked his. It's no big deal."

"No, of course not." Holly's smile said it was a very big deal.

Seriously? Holly may want to play matchmaker for Mrs. Bell, but there wasn't going to be any of that going on for her. She'd missed her chance for a soulmate. She had different goals now and they included both Holly and Ian.

"Shall we, ladies?" Ian held out a hand to both of them.

"Where are we headed?" She waited before clasping his hand. Ian didn't know it yet, but he would be taking a side trip.

He addressed Holly. "I thought we should check in on the Bransons."

Holly's eyes brightened. "Oh yes. They have been together over forty years." She turned to Coco. "You can tell me if they are soulmates."

Coco laughed. "You really like knowing which couples are soulmates, don't you?"

"I do. It makes me happy for them because I know how it felt." Holly's silver glow dimmed a bit with her sadness.

"Did you know many couples have perfectly happy lives even if they aren't soulmates?"

"I'm so glad." Holly sighed with relief. "Since you said not everyone finds theirs, it would be a shame if they couldn't have a great life anyway. I wish you could have found your soulmate."

"I didn't find my soulmate, but I had a great life anyway." She kept the smile on her face and refused to make eye contact with Ian.

Holly looked at her quizzically. "I wonder if you would even know if you saw your soulmate. It might be that you can only see others. For all you know, you may have lived next door to him your whole life."

She'd never thought of that. She'd just assumed she hadn't met him because she thought he was a foreigner for some reason, but maybe he wasn't. It didn't matter now anyway. "You could be right that I may not be able to see my own soulmate, but I can tell you he didn't live next door to me all my life because during my adult life I lived above an ice cream shop and the buildings on either side were stores, and the neighbors next door changed about every two years." She winked.

"Well, I think you wouldn't be allowed to know who your soulmate was. That would be like cheating."

Ian cleared his throat. "So are we ready to move on to the Branson's?" He glanced at each of them as if they were wasting time, and they laughed.

Coco took pity on him for a moment. "Yes, let's see what we can discover on this next visit."

<h1 style="text-align: center;">Chapter Seven</h1>

Ian floated them through town and down a very old side road that had been there since Deervale was first settled. He'd never spent much time in the little village, but he could still appreciate its charm.

He'd left the family home as soon as he could for the city of Glasgow. Even though his father's reach was more than geographical, it still helped to not live in the same building. Attending university and becoming interested in the arts and history from a collector's perspective had given his life some meaning until he met Ella.

He'd never had someone so dependent upon him before. It had been uplifting, proof he could stand on his own two feet. Or so he'd thought.

As they neared the small brick house of the Bransons, he floated the three of them up to phase through the roof. The scene at first looked mundane. Mrs. Branson was on the phone as she sat in her wheelchair in the living room. She smiled as she spoke, her free hand waving in the air.

They found Mr. Branson in the kitchen. He sat at a small table watching the telly, and having a wee dram of Scotch.

"So are they soulmates?" Holly had let go of his hand and addressed Coco.

Coco's usual smile was missing. "They are, but..."

"But what?" Holly floated closer to Mr. Branson. "Is something wrong? He's not going to die soon or anything, is he? Where's the ornament he bought?"

Ian pointed to a small bag on the kitchen counter. "I believe it's right there."

Holly frowned. "I guess he doesn't mean for it to be a surprise." She floated to the doorway to watch Mrs. Branson.

Ian glanced at Coco's face. She understood what was happening. She lifted her gaze to his then looked away. An irrational need to make her smile again filled his psyche. He smothered it.

Coco followed Holly and pointed at the wife. "She's very happy."

Holly nodded.

Coco turned Holly to face Mr. Branson. "What about him?"

They floated closer to the older man.

"Why is he in this room?" Holly's brow reflected her bewilderment. "It's Christmas Eve. Cameron and I would never spend the evening in different rooms. I even wrapped all his presents ahead of time so we could enjoy the evening at Brody's and the night snuggled in our living room." She faced Coco. "We used to stay awake until after midnight just so we could give each other the first kiss of Christmas Day."

Coco looked at him for help. Neither of them were experienced at being married for over sixty years, but they were given an insight that others didn't have or they wouldn't be spirit guides.

He cleared his throat. "I'm afraid that Mrs. Branson has forgotten how important her husband is to her. When she was miserable in her wheelchair, she hated for him to leave her side, but once he bought her the scooter to make her happier, she became so enamored of other people's lives that she has forgotten the one person who loves her unconditionally."

Coco turned teary eyes to Holly. "Mr. Branson is lonely and forgotten."

Holly looked at them and then to Mr. Branson and back to them. "We need to do something about this."

He did enjoy Holly's enthusiasm, but he also anticipated Coco's objections. "What do you propose?"

"Let me think about this." Holly floated into the living room.

He faced Coco, ready for the challenge she would present, but she grabbed his hand and flew them off.

So, she wanted to have their argument away from Holly. If that was her preference, he didn't mind, as long as they weren't alone for too long. He found it much easier to resist her with Holly around. "You have yet to hear what Holly decides upon for a resolution. Or were you planning on deciding for her?"

She glanced at him. "I'm sure whatever she decides you will fully support her then turn on your Scottish charm to convince me otherwise, but I'm on to you now. You can forget that tactic."

Her reminder of his "tactic" had his lips aching to touch hers again. It had been the barest touch because he'd been weak, but it started a need deep in his gut that had merged with his soul's attraction to her warmth. The double enticement was stretching his control toward the breaking point.

The gray ether cleared just seconds before she phased them into a building, but he'd seen two of the words on the sign outside. "Ice cream."

Once inside, Coco let go of his hand and he took a moment to look around. He'd never been to an American ice cream shop before. This one had a stainless-steel counter with round red stools in front of it. There were red booths that lined the walls and round tables with heart-shaped chairs. The walls were shades of pink and one wall sported a mural of ice cream as a landscape with cherry and nut people playing on it.

The whole set up was something out of an old American fifties movie. He brought his gaze back to her. "This is where you used to work."

She shrugged. "Not exactly. I've made it a lot prettier and cleaner. The real deal has ripped stool covers, miss-matched chairs, and well, you get the picture."

He did. She made her space her ideal. She looked ideal in it as well. Still wearing Holly's red velvet robe, she fit in perfectly with the decor. It was her, just like the pink streak in her hair and the tiny candy cane by her eye. Red and pink. Love and sweetness.

Where did that come from?

"I made my place better than it was while I was living. So how come you haven't exchanged the picture of your father with something else, like a landscape or a dried flower arrangement. Shoot, even a naked woman would be better."

A naked— he coughed as the image of a painting of a nude Coco appeared in his head.

"Oh, please. Like you haven't thought of turning that mausoleum you're hanging out in into a major bachelor pad?"

The woman had lost her mind. "I assure you, the thought never—"

She laughed as she solidified and sat on one of the red stools. "I'm just playing with you about the naked woman stuff. But I do want to know why you keep the painting of your dad in your study."

He solidified as well and turned away from her laughter, the sound warming him from the inside out. She was too hard to resist. He strolled over to the mural of the ice cream landscape. "You think I should have something more like this?"

"Of course not. But if you hate your dad so much, why keep his picture up?"

He looked over his shoulder at her and then wished he hadn't. She swiveled back and forth on the stool, the robe revealing much of her legs. He swallowed hard and forced himself to look away. "Who said I hate my father?"

"You did."

He turned back to the mural. "No, I didn't."

"Oh, maybe not in words, but it was implied. My guess is your father was a harsh man and you blame him for whatever didn't go well in your life."

He barked a laugh at that. "Hardly. I take full responsibility for my actions." He spun to face her. "Do you?"

Her eyes widened. "Of course."

Everything about her was comforting, calling him like a siren to drown in the waves of the Mediterranean. She should stay away from him. "So you admit to taking your own life."

She stared in stunned horror for a moment before her brow lowered and she stood. "My own life? I'll have you know I did no such thing. I saved a life. If I could have done so without losing my own I would have." She stalked toward him. "Lynzie had found her soulmate. I hadn't. I couldn't let her life be cut short just as happiness was about to be hers."

He grabbed her by the shoulders. He wanted her to go away or at least hurt as much as he did. It was unfair of him, but she was the one who brought them here. She was determined to burrow underneath his pain and bring his soul's guts to the surface.

He wouldn't let that happen. "And what about your happiness? For all you know, your soulmate was across the street watching."

"You're too cruel." She tried to pull away from him, but he couldn't get his fingers to let go.

"Exactly. That's why my father stares at me every time I'm home." He scowled at her, wanting her to twist away but unable to release her. Wanting her to understand his pain, but refusing to tell her.

Her amber eyes were bright with tears. "Seriously? It's poor rich

Ian and his overbearing father? How pathetically boring." She rolled her eyes. "And here I thought you might actually be interesting. That maybe there was some depth beneath the self-absorbed arrogance. I must be losing my touch."

He barely heard her words, his body too focused on her energy and warmth. The fire in her eyes lit one low in his gut. He tried to fight it. "No." His word barely made it past his lips, but she heard it.

Her eyebrows rose in expectation of an explanation. There was none. He didn't deserve the warmth she exuded, but he craved it as if he were a dying man gasping for one more breath.

"I'm waiting." Her gaze challenged him.

She needed to be taught a lesson. He was not a spirit she could control. He was lost. As he accepted his fate for the thousandth time, he weakened. Pulling her to him, he captured her lips with his own.

Coco struggled against the arms that held her until the desperation of the man communicated itself to her brain. His tongue broke between her lips, searching her mouth like a drowning man searches for a lifeline.

She could no more resist that cry for help than she could resist the hard body making her feel every part a woman. Instead of pushing him away, she grabbed hold of his shirt and pressed her hips to his. Excitement skittered over her skin at the contact with his erection beneath his clothes.

His hold loosened.

No, don't let me go. Her soul recognized his need as more than physical. Moving one hand up, she grabbed hold of his neck and captured his tongue in her mouth.

The deep moan that vibrated his chest sent blood rushing to the juncture of her thighs. His hand buried itself in her hair and grasped her head. His mouth grew insistent, demanding her surrender, and she willing gave in to the cascade of sensation bombarding her body.

His other hand found her ass and he half-lifted her against him, his cock crushed against her mons.

The robe felt stifling, so she tried to move her other hand between them to untie it, but their bodies were too close.

He let go of her head and grabbed her wayward hand, pulling it behind her, his actions neither gentle nor hurtful, but driven with purpose, one she completely agreed with.

Ian's mouth left hers to suck her neck as if he could fill his soul with her own. She released a whimper of need as surrender filled her veins.

He pulled her with him as he backed up and captured both her hands in one of his own, never letting go of her neck.

Before she knew what he was about, his mouth left her and he spun her around, pinning her against the wall, his free hand pushing the robe open to her waist, exposing her breasts to his view.

His gaze riveted to her hard nipples as she took deep breaths, her hands still pinned behind her, her large breasts quivering with her need.

He spoke no words. No compliments left his lips, but his intensity was far more potent. Lifting one large globe with his free hand, he lowered his mouth and sucked.

No gentle foreplay preceded the hard pull on her nipple, nor did she have warning that his teeth would bite just hard enough to cause her sheath to fill with moisture.

She felt wanted by him in every physical way possible as his mouth left one breast for the other. There he bit at her hard peak and licked but didn't suck until his hand had the other nipple firmly between his thumb and forefinger.

Then he squeezed, one with his fingers and the other with his teeth. Her hips pushed toward him of their own accord even as she squealed with pleasure.

There was no finesse as he left her breasts and with his free hand untied the belt that held the rich velvet robe closed. She didn't try to resist his hold on her wrists, afraid that to do so would make him stop. Her instinct said the sexual need he experienced would stop if she tried to take any control by action or word, so she remained silent.

But it was difficult to stay quiet as he pressed his clothed hard body against hers and rocked his cock along her. She wanted to taste him and touch him, but she didn't. His hand around her wrists remained even as his other grabbed her ass and pressed her tighter to him.

She ached to have him fill her, but he didn't unzip his pants. Instead, he kissed her again, his tongue sweeping into her mouth, mimicking the movements of intercourse.

Even as he kept her head pinned against the wall with his kiss, his hips moved back and his free hand roved over her belly to the short soft curls of her pubic hair. Her hands held behind her, caused her pelvis to tilt up, and it was less than a second before his fingers roved over her clit and burrowed between her legs.

His tongue stopped when his fingers encountered the wetness at her entrance. She held her breath, afraid he would leave her wanting him as desperately as he wanted her.

Her readiness must have signaled his own instinct because when he moved his fingers, there was no hesitancy. Two pushed between her folds and speared her.

She cried out, despite his tongue's mastery of her mouth. She bucked her hips, pushing against his fingers, wanting more.

His mouth left hers, giving her much needed air only to clamp down hard on her breast and suck while his fingers pulled out only to thrust back in. She wanted to grasp him to her, hold onto him, but he kept her away, helpless to increase their intimacy.

He rose against her again, his fingers buried deep inside her, his hard body pressing her against the wall, but this time he looked at her.

His eyes were dark to almost black and glazed over. It reminded her of a tiger she'd seen on television and she shuddered at the wildness. His fingers inside her played, scissoring back and forth, his palm rubbing against her clit.

As she stood there pinned and at his mercy, she realized he wanted her to come. No, he needed her to. That sliver of insight relaxed her final reservations. As she stared straight up at him, her head bent back so she could make eye contact, she opened her mouth, inviting him to take her.

Ian's eyes widened a fraction before a growl rose from deep in his chest and his mouth came down on hers. His fingers pulled from her sheath.

She whimpered at the loss, but in an instant, the head of his cock pushed between her legs, past her sensitized clit and slid into her opening.

Sparks ignited between her thighs and flowed outward. Ian didn't move as if being buried inside her was a lifelong dream he'd finally realized.

But he growled again, this time against her neck as he sucked. When his hand let go of her wrists, she moved her arms to pull him toward her, loving how full she felt. But he grabbed both her hands and lifted them over her head, once more capturing them together.

It took everything she had not to struggle and wait for him to start the rhythm that would satisfy them both. His mouth came away from her neck and he licked her ear. The tingles from that traveled down to her core and her sheath tightened around him.

She felt him bend his legs before he angled himself between her thighs and slid her up the wall, his cock hitting her cervix. Her shout of pleasure and surprise seemed to release him. Letting go of her hands, he grasped her ass as she wound her legs around his waist.

He thrust into her, sliding her against the wall until he pulled out again. His need was animalistic but she didn't care. Every time he filled her body, a torrent of pleasure overwhelmed her. She simply held on as he pushed her higher and tighter until every molecule of her being burst with joy.

Light filled her soul and she floated on air. She'd never thought that before while solid. Far more than satisfaction filled her. Happiness like she'd never known buzzed through her.

She opened her eyes. Her head rested on Ian's shoulder. It made for a large pillow but it was still clothed.

Her conscience told her she'd done the right thing, but it could make their assignment a little awkward…unless he opened up. Now that they had shared, well, not really shared. More like he took, but she wasn't complaining because it felt so amazing.

She kissed his neck and his head jerked up. His gray gaze was back to stormy and he looked disoriented. Maybe she felt that good. She gave him a shy smile. "That was fantastic."

He blinked before he looked away, his frown already forming.

She grabbed his face and made him look at her. "There is nothing wrong with what we just did. Be happy."

He jerked his head from her hands and pulled out of her body, letting her down carefully, but he immediately walked away.

Oh boy, this wasn't good. Wrapping the robe around her, she strode by him so she could face him. "Tell me you enjoyed that."

He raised his stupid eyebrow, but didn't say anything.

Placing her hands on her hips, she frowned at him. "Well?"

He shook his head. "I apologize. That will never happen again."

What? She wanted to pound on his chest and make him talk, show emotion, anything. Instead, she took a deep breath. "There's nothing wrong with taking a little pleasure now and then. The afterlife is supposed to be about that, not all work. One of the perks of being able to travel through time is that we can enjoy."

"No!" He barked the word as if it slipped out accidently.

Oh. There was something else going on here. "Are you angry that you found pleasure?"

"I brought you pleasure. I did not seek fulfillment for myself."

Seriously? If he'd just speak plainly maybe she wouldn't have to pepper him with so many—oh. He didn't have an orgasm. She flushed that she'd been so caught up in her own pleasure, she hadn't paid attention to what he was feeling besides that desperate need to be with her.

She was more than a little confused now.

"I suggest we return to Holly and the Bransons." His matter of fact tone seemed out of place after what just happened. How could he be so emotional one moment and so distant the next. She wasn't like that.

"If you don't mind, I'd like to take a minute. I just had a wonderful experience and I need to regroup." She couldn't quite manage a smile. The whole event too far out of her realm of knowledge.

He nodded. "I understand. I will be there when you wish to resume."

"Wait, Ian."

He phased just as she grabbed his arm and her hand went through him. The jolt of the contact made her shiver.

He floated through the ceiling while she found a stool and sat hard. Part of her wanted to rejoice over getting Ian to open up physically, if not emotionally, but the other part of her felt as if she'd just been dumped.

Why did she have to always try to help people? Cameron never said Ian was her case, though he did intimate that Ian needed her. She snorted. Probably hadn't expected Ian to need her in the way he just had though.

She spun around on the stool. "I need a hot fudge sundae with rocky road ice cream after that work out."

The sundae appeared in front of her, complete with whip cream and cherry the way she liked it. She sighed. "A spoon and napkin would help."

As the two items materialized next to the ice cream, she picked up the spoon. Maybe after she recuperated, she could think clearly again about both Ian and Holly.

Ian flew to his study. As soon as he arrived, he solidified and strode to the kitchen. Taking out two bottles of ale, he opened them and went back to his desk.

What the fuck had he done? He took a swig and sat the bottle down. He should have resisted. What happened? When did his control slip?

When he let his emotions get the better of him. All Coco's fire and warm sweet scent.

Fuck, he still smelled her. She was on his clothes, his skin. He smelled the shoulder of his shirt. The familiar scent was tantalizing, but he still couldn't name it. Even now his body reacted, not that his erection had relaxed. Being inside her warmth was heaven. He didn't deserve that.

He took another gulp of ale. At least he'd had the presence of mind, or gut instinct, to deny himself fulfillment. What a cluster fuck that would have been. Coco was tough. She might be warm, friendly, and smart but she was tough. She'd be fine. He was the one who was wrecked.

She'd tasted so good. Smelled so good. Felt better than anything he remembered while alive. If he'd met her maybe he could have had a decent life.

What was he thinking? Poor Ella. She needed him and he'd let her down. He should have been there. He should have made her feel safe and secure.

The vision of Ella's face being covered with the blanket froze him. He'd stood back, letting her family take her away. *You should have been there. We counted on you to take care of our baby.*

He gulped the last of the ale and threw it across the room. They said the signs were there. She'd been too happy that day. Too normal. He should have known. He should have stopped her. How could he have loved her and not known she was so unhappy?

Because, you asshole, you didn't love her, not enough. And still you seek warmth, light, sweetness. Do you never learn? He picked up the full bottle of ale and saluted his father. "See what a mess your screwed-up son is? You much prefer me this way, don't you?" He heaved the full bottle at the painting.

The ale splashed as the glass shattered and fell to the floor. In Ian's head, he heard his father laughing at him.

"Screw this." He stepped up to the fireplace and grabbed the brass poker. He hooked the instrument into the center of the painting and tore through it.

Something shifted. He wasn't sure if it was the room or himself and he didn't care. Tearing through the painting two more times, he stared at what should have been a blank wall behind it.

But there was a mural on it. The tears revealed a female leg, much like the Ruben that hung in the spirit guide lounge.

Curiosity distracted him from his childish rant, and he waved his hand to rid himself of his father's portrait.

He froze. Before him in all her naked glory was Coco Baker, painted by Ruben. It couldn't be.

"Shoot, even a naked woman would be better." Coco's words came back to haunt him, but she was right. She lay on a bed of rumpled sheets, what looked like a 12-point buck kneeling next to her as she pet its head. On the table beside her was a golden chalice and above her were two cupid boys. In the background, a door was ajar and two eyes spied on her, the bare lines of a man's goatee visible in the shadows.

The picture drew him. He touched the knee of the woman, the only place he could reach in his solid form. The scent of warm chocolate filled his nostrils and he pulled his hand back.

Coco was his temptation and he'd already failed. More torture. More punishment. Well deserved.

He sat in the recliner placed before the fireplace, tilted it back and stared at the painting. Coco's skin had been soft and full of curves that called to him. Her pure ecstasy had been beautiful and bringing her to orgasm filled his soul with light for a brief moment. If he could come inside her, with her, it would be like nothing else in existence.

She was unique, like no woman he'd ever met. Her easy smile, need to help, keen insights drew him to her. She was the light to his dark. Her guilt free existence was irresistible. If he could have one wish, it would be that Coco meet her soulmate. She deserved that.

And he deserved his punishment. He'd already proven himself weak. He couldn't resist her. What if next time he let himself get lost in her? Would his torture be that much worse? For the first time, he resented his penance. How long would he suffer because he couldn't keep the woman he loved from killing herself?

"Fuck." He stood. It wasn't his place to question. His opportunity to act had come and gone. He admitted he was weak. He had to get off this assignment.

Phasing, Ian floated through the ceiling of his study and directly into Cameron's office.

Cameron appeared to be waiting for him and it was clear his supervisor was not happy.

"Are you done?"

He crossed his arms. "I have no idea what you're referring to."

Cameron slammed the book he'd been writing in down on the desk and rose. "I'm referring to your half-assed approach to this assignment. And what the fuck is Coco thinking? Has she completely lost it?"

Ian's initial irritation at his work being called less than stellar paled in comparison to the anger that knotted his stomach when Cameron belittled Coco. "What are you talking about?"

His supervisor threw up his hands. "I'm talking about Coco's obvious plan to turn my wife into the town gossip. She's got Holly panting at the bit to meddle in everyone else's affairs. First Luca then Mrs. Bell and now the Bransons?" Cameron stepped in front of him. "What's next? A fund for Sophia's sister?"

He stood his ground, surprised Cameron had been spying on them. What else had he seen? "You've been watching?"

Cameron's jaw worked before he answered through gritted teeth. "She's my wife!"

He'd never seen the man so out of sorts. "I believe we are showing Holly there is more to life in Deervale than the four walls of her Christmas shop. That *is* what you requested."

"*Our* Christmas shop. I want her to join the living, not get intimately involved in everyone else's lives. I want her to live her *own* life. I sent Coco with you so you wouldn't mess this up, but she's just made it worse."

Ian dropped his arms, balling his hands into fists. He didn't give a shit what Cameron thought of him, but to dismiss Coco as incompetent crossed a line he didn't know he had. "Coco's work has been stellar."

Cameron snorted. "Hardly. Either fix this or neither of you will ever have another assignment. I promise you that."

Chapter Eight

Coco sat in the lounge contemplating her root beer when her friend walked in. Joy was a spirit of Christmas Future and the purest of all of them. Sometimes Coco felt a bit frumpy next to Joy's put together appearance, but she was such a sweet soul, she made everyone comfortable. Coco waved.

Joy joined her. "What happened to that beautiful dress you were wearing earlier?"

Coco looked down at her jeans and red Christmas long-sleeved t-shirt with Cindy Lou Who on it. "I traded with my client who was wearing a robe. I thought a pair of jeans was a bit better apparel for work."

"I would agree. Do I dare ask?"

Coco shook her head. "Let's just say that it has a lot to do with Ian Fergusson."

Joy's smile faltered. That was so rare that Coco tensed. Maybe she shouldn't pry into Ian's life after all. Then again, it was a bit too late for that. She'd already discovered what happened in the Glasgow flat thanks to a rather talkative Mrs. Ferrisletter.

"How can I help you?"

Coco cocked her head. "I figured out, or I think I have, why Ian Fergusson is so distant. He blames himself for not saving his suicidal fiancée."

Joy's smile was sad.

"I also discovered that not only did her family blame him, but his own family did as well, and the whole tragedy was covered in the press, who also blamed him."

"It was a tragic event for all involved."

Coco nodded in agreement, crushing her need to defend Ian. She didn't have enough information yet to do that.

Joy sat patiently waiting. Coco was almost afraid to ask, but she just had to know. "Could you tell me, if Ella hadn't met Ian, would she still be alive today?"

Joy shook her head. "Oh my, no. Ella would have taken her own life no matter who she was with. She had a severe chemical imbalance and though the medications that were prescribed for her worked, they also put her in a haze."

Coco's hope grew. "She didn't like taking them, I gather?"

"Not like it?" Joy leaned in to whisper. "She flushed her medicine down the toilet so her family wouldn't know she skipped it." Joy sat straight again. "It was a matter of time for Ella. The poor dear was terribly unhappy. I don't understand why some people have to be born with such a weight to bear."

She didn't understand it either, but she was unashamedly more worried about Ian. "So Ian isn't being punished for what happened?"

"What?" Joy's eyes rounded. "No one here is punished. We are here because we have the potential to still help the living. Why would you think Ian is being punished?"

More to the point, why did Ian feel that.

"Coco, are you interested in Ian?" Joy's look was cautious.

"You mean because he's an arrogant asshole who's friendly to no one?"

Her friend laughed, the sound like the gurgling of a small brook as the water wound between the stones. "I see you are quite aware of his personality."

She rolled her eyes. "That and then some. I'm interested because I'm working on a case with him." She lowered her voice. "It's Cameron's wife."

Joy's smile froze and worry entered her gaze. "Be careful."

"You mean because the last sprit guides to help Cameron's wife disappeared?"

Joy nodded. "There are dozens of rumors floating around. One that the new girl, Jessica, turned into a ghost and another that the trainer, Duncan, simply ceased to exist because he'd been here for so long."

Coco frowned at that. "I didn't think there was a time limit. I thought we are here forever."

Joy shrugged. "I'm just repeating what I've heard. I don't know."

"Since I have you, can you tell me anything about my future?"

Joy touched her cheek. "You know I can't see the future of spirit guides."

Coco gave her friend a shrewd look. "Can't or won't?"

"Can't." Joy shook her head. "I'm really glad I can't. I'm not sure I'd want to know what's ahead for all of eternity. I think that would be a bit overwhelming."

She'd never thought of that, then again she'd always been a Spirit of Christmas Present, so the other positions and their abilities hadn't occurred to her. "You're right. I'm just happy you could give me a little insight about what I'm dealing with. Thank you." She gave Joy a hug.

"You know I'm happy to help anytime, just be careful. If you're unsure about anything, ask Cameron."

Coco stood. "I will. Now, I need to go find one arrogant spirit and continue our assignment." As soon as she stepped back from Joy, another spirit guide engaged the woman in conversation and Coco quickly left.

Joy's information energized her. Now she wanted to confirm one more piece of the puzzle that was Ian Fergusson, and she could give her whole attention to Holly. Phasing out of the lounge, she came through the door of Cameron's office and solidified.

Cameron and Ian stood nose to nose, both with hands balled into fists, though to be fair, Ian was once again just a bit taller. The tension in the room was ridiculous and it sent shivers across her skin.

She wasn't sure what bothered her more, that her boss was angry at Ian or that Ian was obviously being stubborn about something, but in either case, it came back to him.

"What's going on here?" She strode forward and pushed her way between the two towers.

Ian, as usual, didn't say a word, so she looked to Cameron.

Her boss gave Ian a final "I'm warning you" look and turned toward his desk. "Nothing. We're done."

She placed her hands on her hips. "Good because I need to speak with you."

Cameron shook his head. "No, what you need to do is get back to my wife. I'm not happy about how things are progressing."

What the frick? "What do you mean? They are going beautifully. I expect Holly will be visiting her family next year, possibly go out of her way to be a friend to Sophia, and even celebrate Christmas with others. To me that's pretty good progress so far."

Cameron didn't look at her. He stared at Ian. "It's not enough."

"What?"

Ian's hand on her shoulder stopped her from continuing. "Let's go."

She looked up at him and for once his gaze wasn't cold. He was furious but not with her, and boy was she glad. If looks could kill, someone would be…dead?

She glanced back at Cameron, but Ian phased her and flew them out of the office.

"You're going to have to tell me what that was about either now or later."

His hand on her shoulder tightened but he didn't respond. Normally, that would piss her off, but she had the feeling he was barely holding everything in. Having him explode as they arrived at the Bransons wouldn't be such a good thing.

"Okay, later it is." She grinned as his hold on her loosened. She sneaked a peek at him to see his face was still just as hard as before, but then again, the man didn't know how to relax. Even when they had sex, he was tense or rather intense.

Her body responded instantly to the memory. She wouldn't deny it. She found him sexually attractive and she wanted more. She'd come to that conclusion over her sundae. Now what she craved was to see him completely naked. Hmm, that might be one way to get to the bottom of Ian's guilt too. She liked that idea a lot.

They phased into the Bransons' kitchen just as Holly turned from watching the wife talk on the phone. "I have an idea on—you changed."

Coco looked at her own clothes and quirked her lip. "I was hoping you wouldn't mind trading that dress for your robe. I've grown very attached to it." Did she just hear Ian take a deep breath? She hoped so.

Holly waved her away. "Of course. I bought it online last year. But this dress is awesome."

"You'll have to have it taken in a little."

Holly winked. "Or I can eat more."

Coco flushed. She'd never been "fat" per se, but she did carry a little extra weight.

"I think Coco's size is perfect for her and your size is perfect for you." Ian's serious voice coming from behind her made her more uncomfortable because it reminded her of exactly how much of her he'd seen…and tasted.

She refocused on Holly, her boss's reprimand still ringing in her ears. "I'm glad you don't mind a trade. So, what idea do you have?"

"What do you think of this?" Holly floated toward them. "You make me solid and I'll call up Mrs. Branson and pretend I think it's her husband and just gush over him like I saw him in the market and would really like to meet for coffee. There's nothing like a little jealousy to make Mrs. Branson remember what a great guy she has."

"You are quite the minx." Coco loved the idea, but still didn't like making Holly solid. "I would just tweak that plan a bit."

Holly's eyes lit with excitement. "Okay."

"I suggest you do that tomorrow, when you're home for Christmas. It's not like you have any other plans besides calling your family in America."

Holly squirmed. "But that's Christmas day. It might not be so believable."

"You can pretend to be checking on Mr. Branson to see if he has a place to go for Christmas dinner."

Holly nodded, but she looked to Ian.

Coco bit her lip and waited for Ian to tell Holly he'd unphase her right now, just like last time.

"I agree with Coco."

At his words, she spun to face him. "You do?"

"I do." He didn't elaborate, but that was nothing new.

Holly floated to Ian. "Are you two ganging up on me?" She said it with a half-smile.

"No." He looked at her and she swore there was appreciation in his eyes. "It's simply the right thing to do."

Coco blinked. She had to be mistaken.

Holly sighed. "Another thing on my to-do list for *after* I'm home."

Coco put her arm around her. "It's not that long of a list and all of it is fun. Look at it this way. You have some fun meddling in your future."

Holly nodded but it was clear she wasn't convinced.

"Tell you what." Coco glanced at Ian hoping he wouldn't argue with her. "Why don't we go visit Ethan? I believe he's about to get ready for Brody's party."

Holly frowned.

"What? You don't want to see Ethan? I thought you'd like to see Cameron's best friend as well as Brody for that matter."

Ian floated forward and turned Holly's face to look at them. "They are too close to Cameron."

Holly wouldn't meet their gazes and Coco's own heart hurt. "Didn't Brody invite you to the party?" She knew he had, but didn't want Holly to know that.

"Yes, but…."

Ian folded his arms. "But what?"

She didn't look at him, instead she spoke to the floor. "I promised Jessica and Duncan that I would try and accept any future invitations, but after last Christmas, no more came." She shrugged. "I guess after turning them down for a whole year, they just gave up until today."

Coco smiled. "So they did invite you."

Holly finally met her gaze. "Yes, but why now? I'll tell you why. Now, at this time of the year, they pity me."

Oh boy, this young woman couldn't get out of her own way. "Then it sounds like now is a great time to find out how they really feel."

"I already know—"

"Holly." Ian's tone was that of a father scolding a child and as much as Coco resented him using it, it did have the desired effect.

"Well, if you insist. Are you sure you two agree on this?" Holly's hope that they didn't was too obvious.

Coco looked at Ian. "Ethan's?"

He nodded, but a glimmer of amusement sparked in his eyes.

For the first time, she felt they were truly a team and she loved the feeling. Oh. Another puzzle piece snapped into place. This one for her.

Ian floated between the two women and grasped their hands. If anyone would take the fall for his and Coco's failure with Holly, he would. He had a new goal now in addition to helping his supervisor's wife to his satisfaction. Ian was determined to protect Coco no matter the outcome.

There was something strange about the way Cameron attacked their work. He wasn't sure, but something didn't feel right, almost like Cameron had a plan, possibly to be rid of them and started the confrontation to justify a later outcome with his superiors. That is what put Ian on high alert now.

He brought the women through the ceiling of Ethan Stewart's family home. It was a good-sized home for the area, but only a fraction of his own. From what he knew of this young man, he could be a good friend to Holly and might constitute what Cameron considered, "living her own life."

Ethan sat on a dark brown couch in a parlor tying his shoes. He was in the prime of his life with broad shoulders, curly hair and wide set eyes. His movements were measured as if he went through life cautiously.

"Ian." Coco's scared whisper jolted him.

He let go of Holly's hand to turn to Coco. "What is it?" The fear in her eyes had him squeezing her hand harder.

She leaned closer, her sweet scent filling his nostrils. "Not here." She glanced at Holly.

In an instant, he brought them into the ether. "What is it? You're afraid."

She tried to smile but it was pathetic. He could actually feel her hand shaking. He let go and held her shoulders. "Tell me."

"It's Ethan."

"What about him?"

"He's her soulmate."

He frowned. "Who's soulmate?"

She rolled her eyes. "Holly's who else's? The minute we phased in, I noticed Ethan's golden glow. I didn't see anyone else in the room, so I was confused. I turned to ask you if you could see anyone else and that's when I saw Holly's silver glow had changed to golden. He's another soulmate for her."

Ian's stomach tightened. Fuck. "This isn't good."

Coco's eyes were wide. "I know. What will Cameron think? But how can it be bad? He's her soulmate."

He couldn't care less who was whose soulmate. What concerned him was what Cameron would do to Coco if she told him. The anger he'd witnessed earlier was far from rational. "Maybe you're mistaken."

She pulled out from under his hands to put her own on her hips. "Excuse me? I'm not mistaken. Holly is suddenly glowing golden and the only difference is that she's in the same room as Ethan."

He folded his arms. He hadn't expected this turn of events. "But if the two of them don't know they are soulmates, then there's no reason to expect them to find each other. After all, Holly is avoiding him like the plague."

Coco dropped her arms. "But soulmates should at least meet. They are meant to be together."

"They've already met." He took a deep breath and made a tough call. "Don't tell her."

He could see the struggle in Coco's eyes. He couldn't begin to comprehend what it would be like to have a gift such as hers.

However, he could imagine people discovering it and bothering her all the time. That she felt an obligation was clear.

He floated toward her and cupped her face in his hands. "I know this is hard, but for this visit, keep it a secret between you and me."

She searched his eyes, and he willed her to take heed to his guidance.

"Okay. For now."

He gave her a small smile and kissed her nose. But the softness of her skin against his palms and the sweet chocolaty scent that filled his senses made her lips too irresistible. Lowering his face, he kissed her gently, determined to show her he cared about her, though he had no clue when that had happened.

Her tongue willingly met his, and if time were a factor he'd swear it was less than a micro second before every part of his body came alive from his tiniest blood capsule to his largest muscle. Even his brain zeroed in on her, wanting her, needing her, lov—He jerked his head back.

Coco took a deep breath and slowly opened her eyes. "I'm really glad you're my partner on this case."

Her amber gaze was honest, making it clear she meant every word and not only because it was a difficult assignment but because she liked him.

A tiny flame of hope kindled in his chest and he tried to smother it, but the light inside him was far too hard to resist. He simply wasn't strong enough, and in his heart, he feared that would be his final downfall. "Are you ready to see what we can teach Holly with this visit to Ethan?"

Coco nodded, and he forced himself to float away from her, but he took her hand and brought them back where they had left.

Holly pointed to Ethan as he looked at his watch before grabbing up his coat. "It's hard to believe he and Cam got along so well. Ethan was the quiet one. More hesitant. He needed to look at all sides of a decision, collect all the facts, and determine all possible ramifications before making a move. It drove Cam crazy." Holly smiled fondly. "But he loved Ethan like a brother. He often told me that Ethan saved his neck a dozen times and if he'd listened to him more often, he would have stayed out of a lot of trouble."

Holly's smile disappeared. "If Ethan had been with Cam the day he died, Cam would probably be alive today."

Coco floated over and put her arm around Holly.

Ian made himself stay where he was. "If Cam ignored Ethan's advice on a regular basis, I doubt that Ethan's presence would have changed the outcome."

"He does have a point." Coco squeezed Holly. "Besides, nothing can change the past. You can only control your future."

Since Ethan took that moment to walk out of the room, the three of them followed him through a dining room and into a large but comfortable kitchen with warm oak cabinets and a table to match.

Ethan kissed his mother on the cheek as she opened a cupboard and took out a bag of flavored crisps. "I thought you were headed to the Campbells, Mum?"

"Oh aye, but the MacDonalds are coming here first for a wee scran before we motor over. And what aboot you? Are you going to Brody's now?"

Ethan snatched an orange from the counter, threw his coat over the back of a chair and sat at the kitchen table. "I am, but I don't want to arrive too early or Brody will make me entertain while he finishes helping Sarah set up. He's never ready for these things."

His mum agreed as she set up a plate with crisps and hard bread sticks. "Don't you need to give a certain someone a lift?"

Ethan peeled the orange on a napkin as he spoke. "No. She's not going."

His mum stopped preparing the plate and faced him. "Did you ask her?"

He shook his head. "Ethan Alexander James Stewart why not? How's she going to know how you feel about her if you don't talk to her?"

Ethan stuffed an orange slice in his mouth to avoid answering.

Holly's eyes rounded. "Holy crap, Ethan likes someone! This is wonderful!" She turned toward them. "Cam and I despaired of him ever falling for someone. He goes on a date or two but usually just to have someone to take to a party. He even took Cam's cousin, Brooke, to Brody's one year. I think she liked him, but it wasn't mutual."

Holly looked straight at Coco. "If I find out who he likes, maybe I could arrange a chance meeting. If the two were in the same room, you could tell me if they were soulmates, right?"

Coco swallowed hard. "Yes, I could, but I won't be here past tonight."

"Oh right. You seem so real to me. I forget I won't see you on Christmas day." Holly looked back at Ethan.

His mother pulled out the chair opposite of him. "Ethan, there be no such thing as getting your ducks in a row when it comes to love. You just have to jump in with both feet and see where it takes you."

Ethan stuffed another orange slice in his mouth and chewed.

Ian could see Coco was worried about what Ethan might say next. He pulled her hand into his. She gave him the pathetic smile she used when trying to appear as if all was well when it wasn't.

Holly floated closer to Ethan, looking for clues. "Come on, spill it already."

As if he'd heard her, he finally swallowed. "She's not ready yet."

"Exactly how many years are you going to let go by before telling her how you feel?" His mum put her hand flat down on the able. "What if she's not interested? You'll have wasted your prime. I say tell her and see what happens. I can't imagine her not loving my lad, but if she doesn't then you can move on to someone else."

Ethan's mum rose from the table and went back to preparing for her guests, but all three of them saw Ethan mouth the words. *There will never be another.*

"Oh, did you see that?" Holly pointed at Ethan. "We have to find out who he loves. We *have* to."

Coco's grip on his hand had tightened considerably. He could tell it was all she could do not to say something to Holly. It was time to distract his charge. "I think that's an excellent plan. Weren't you invited to Ethan's parents' home for Christmas dinner?"

Holly frowned. "Stop patronizing me. You probably already know I was invited, and I turned it down."

He shrugged. "Wouldn't that have been a great opportunity to quiz Ethan on his love life."

"Great. You made your point. Next year I'll accept *all* Christmas invitations. Will that make you happy?" Holly's lower lip protruded out just a tad, making her appear the child he was accused of treating her like.

"The question is, will it make *you* happy."

Holly sighed and floated to Coco. "You know, I think I liked it better when the two of you didn't agree so much."

Coco did smile at that. "Don't worry, I'm sure there's plenty more of that to come."

He doubted that. If he wasn't mistaken, one more visit should do it for them. "Shall we move on then?"

From the look on Coco's face, he was sure Cameron Douglas just materialized behind him and he looked over his shoulder. But no one was there.

"Ian."

Now what? There was that tone of hers. "Yes."

Coco frowned at him. "I think we need to discuss this."

He raised an eyebrow. "Very well."

"Oh good." Holly grinned. "You two go outside and argue. I'm going to stay here and see if Ethan reveals anything else."

He shook his head. For as smart as Holly was, she just didn't understand the concept of traveling through time. If he and Coco left, they would return before Holly took her next breath.

Coco grabbed his arm and sped them through space and time. "Oh shoot, I miscalculated."

They phased into what must be her apartment over the ice cream shop. He guessed that because he recognized Holly's robe thrown over a chair in the living room. The image of Coco with the robe splayed open clouded his vision. He took a deep breath, but the space smelled of Coco and he closed his eyes.

"I know. The place is a mess, but that's how I like it."

At her voice, he opened his eyes to find she had solidified. She stood next to a long red sofa that sported a purple afghan and violet throw pillows. The glass coffee table had a number of magazines splayed over it and two pansy coasters.

"It took me a while to get things left where I wanted them. I like the feel of this much better than clean and sterile."

He snorted silently. She'd just described his home.

"Okay, so say something." Coco stood with her arms folded over her ample chest, a look of uncertainty in her gaze, but a defensive lift to her chin was also apparent.

He scanned the rest of the area, the open kitchen had canisters and utensils covering the counters, but arranged neatly. And through the door to a bedroom he could see rumpled sheets. To get her bed to be left unmade must have taken persistence. Then again, he didn't doubt her ability to make it happen.

To distract himself from how those sheets must feel, he answered her. "It's homey. Is that not what you wanted it to be?"

She let out an exasperated sigh and dropped her hands. "I

guess it doesn't matter what you think of my space. It's not as if I cared for yours."

He solidified and raised his brow, but didn't comment.

Coco strode into her kitchen and went to a cabinet. When she came back into the living room, she handed him a drink. He sniffed it. "Scotch?"

She nodded and flopped down on the sofa. "Why not? You're Scottish, our boss is Scottish and our assignment is in Scotland. I'm the only fish out of water here, so as they say, when in Rome…" She tipped her glass and took a sip. "Whoa, that's potent."

He sniffed at his Scotch. "It's single malt and a high caliber one at that. Thank you." He took a sip and let it flow over his tongue. It had to be at least a hundred years old.

"We need to talk about Cameron."

Surprised by her choice of topic, he sat down on the matching recliner. "Why Cameron?"

She shook her head. "Because I need your advice on how best to approach him about his wife having another soulmate. I mean, those two have one of those special love bonds. It's going to kill him to know she could have that with another, and his best friend at that."

The Scotch aftertaste that he savored but a moment ago turned sour in his mouth. "You're right. Cameron is not going to take this well." Maybe he wouldn't take it at all. Ian's gut tightened. This wouldn't end well. "We could simply not tell him."

Coco rolled her eyes. "Seriously?"

He shook his head. "No, it is significant enough that he must be told. I will handle it."

Coco sprayed her Scotch from her mouth. "Excuse me? I don't think so. I'm the one who recognizes soulmates, not you. And Cameron knows I have this ability, so there's no other option. I have to tell him. I just want your opinion on the best approach."

His hand reflectively tightened around his glass. "No."

"What do you mean, 'no'. You have no say in this. It's my responsibility."

Ian couldn't shake the feeling that if Coco told Cameron, the man would turn berserker on her, far worse than his anger when he accused them of failing at the assignment. Ian didn't want to see Coco come to harm, punished, or disappear. He slowly put down his glass and stared at her.

Fuck, she was beautiful, warm, full of energy and light. He couldn't let that be snuffed out. He was already punished for failing one woman. It was only fitting he be punished in saving another. "I will tell Cameron. There is a chance, based on the conversation he and I last had that he will hurt you."

"Hurt me? What do you mean?"

There was no clear explanation. "As you heard, Cameron is not happy with our progress. There's a possibility he could cause you to…to cease to exist." He held up his hand as she opened her mouth to interrupt. "Let me finish. He was *that* angry when I met with him, and even borderline unstable. He is extremely protective of his wife. If I tell him the news, there is a good chance he'll take his initial anger out on me."

Coco set her glass on the coffee table. "But that wouldn't be fair. It's my gift. I need to tell him."

Ian rose, too agitated to sit anymore. He needed to make her see. "You can, but let me take his anger first. If I disappear, no one will be the poorer for it. But if you, if you— you are needed and loved. You are important to the spirit guide world."

Her eyes grew wide with disbelief. "I can't believe your saying this? What makes you think you're expendable? That's what you're saying, isn't it? You're expendable?"

He paced to the windows that looked out onto main street USA and turned to stare her down. "I am. I'm only here to be punished for failing to save the woman I loved. Maybe by sacrificing myself for you, I can find some peace."

"Ian Fergusson, how dare you? Have you no respect for yourself at all? Do you take no pride in the living children you've helped while here? You may not be liked, a situation you go out of your way to cultivate, but you do a lot of good and you are not expendable."

He strode to her. "I have to do this. Don't you see? This is a chance for me to redeem myself."

Coco rose, her face hard, her eyes glittering. "You idiot, you don't have to redeem yourself! You didn't do anything wrong, except maybe love the wrong woman." She glared at him. "I very much doubt you were Ella's soulmate."

His gut tightened into a knot. "What do you know about Ella?"

"A lot more than you. For example, I know that had she never met you, she still would have committed suicide."

What the fuck? He should have known Coco would spy on his past. She just couldn't keep her nose out of other people's business. He worked his jaw to make it function. "You can't know that. Whether I was her soulmate or not, I could have saved her. It doesn't matter if she would have killed herself if she wasn't with me. The fact is, she may well have lived a fulfilling life with me if I could have just shown her how much I loved her!"

His chest tightened making it hard to breathe. His whole body wanted to smash something at his complete helplessness over Ella's fate.

Coco scowled. "Maybe you couldn't show her how much you loved her because no one could have loved her enough. Why can't you see that? You keep punishing yourself for something you had no control over. Ella would have found a way whether you loved her enough or not."

He fisted his hands, forcing himself to stay where he was or he might break something of hers. What was he afraid of? Nothing truly broke here, which in of itself was more of the torture. "I'm not punishing myself. This—" He swung his arm wide, breaking the window with his fist, the instant of pain and blood disappeared as quickly as it came, frustrating him further. "This place is my punishment."

He stared at her. "You are my punishment."

Chapter Nine

Ian strode across the room and grabbed Coco by her shoulders. "You are my temptation. You've tortured me more than anything else here."

She pushed him away and he released her.

"You're more messed up than I thought." Coco pointed to her temple. "This is all in your head. We're here to help the living because deep down, despite our failings, we are *good* people."

He sneered. "Really? If we're so good, then why aren't we in paradise?" He raised his eyebrow. "I'll tell you why. Because I failed the one person who depended on me and you failed to find your soulmate."

"What? I had no control over finding my soulmate. I know that because I'm the one who has the gift of recognition."

He folded his arms over his chest. "But you did know he was foreign, yet you never did anything to put yourself in a place where you might meet him. Just like Holly not visiting her parents, you refused to act."

She closed her mouth, but her eyes widened with doubt and he hated himself even more. She didn't deserve to be saddled with him. Cameron should have known better. At the thought of his superior, he phased.

"What are you going to do now? Go home to sulk?" Coco phased as well as if she'd follow him.

Fuck. "No. I'm going to Cameron to get off this case, one way or another. I'd rather cease to exist than continue it."

Coco froze and blinked twice in shock.

He flew through her ceiling, his insides swirling with a need he couldn't satisfy. He wanted more than anything to believe her, bury himself in her body and forget his life.

But he wasn't that selfish. If she wouldn't save herself from him and Cameron, he would.

Coco's heart stopped, paralyzing her entire body. She couldn't even solidify. She completely believed Ian would offer himself up as the sacrifice.

The second her heart lurched at the thought of that, he started to glow golden. She couldn't even look down at herself, but she knew.

He was her soulmate. How could he be her soulmate?

Tears formed in her eyes and her body loosened. She solidified, but continued to stand in the middle of her living room, stunned.

Ian was her soulmate.

No. Yes. How?

She dropped onto her couch, still trying to grasp that concept. Arrogant asshole himself? Why wouldn't she have known the minute they met. Something weird was going on.

Had the glow been repressed because she didn't like him? Because they were now in the afterlife? Did that change how her gift worked. She'd never seen any glows among her fellow spirit guides or trainers.

Even Cameron didn't glow.

Then why had Ian? Ian! She sat up. Her heart hurting with the knowledge he would do anything to be released from their assignment. She had to stop him.

Despite her anxiety, she didn't move. What if this was a trick? What if it was the beginning of how the two of them would disappear? How could a man who punished himself be her soulmate?

Even if he was, was she strong enough to handle that? The utter belief he had that he was the cause of Ella's death was unshakeable. She couldn't love a man who didn't love himself. Who punished himself.

Is this how her best friend Lynzie had felt? Had she made Lynzie miserable by making her promise to stay with her soulmate? What if her own ultimate sacrifice had been totally wrong? She shivered, the thought too harsh to accept.

She stood. She didn't trust the sudden glow anyway. It could even be Cameron playing tricks on her and if he was, he would hear about it.

No, she couldn't love Ian. Could she?

She shook her head. No, but she could keep him from doing something stupid, like pissing off their boss. Phasing, she flew out into the ether of space and time to Cameron's office.

When she arrived, she hesitated outside his door, solidifying first. Ian's observations about Cameron's protectiveness of his wife scared her. She swallowed then knocked on the door.

"Come in."

She'd be nice and polite and see if she could discover what Cameron was up to. Opening the door, she half expected Ian to be there, but the room was empty.

"Coco." Cameron's smile was reassuring, but she didn't let her guard down.

"I had a few questions about our case, do you mind?" She still hovered by the door.

Cameron stood. "Of course. Come sit."

She took a deep breath, Ian's words coupled with the knowledge that the last two spirit guides assigned to Cameron's wife had disappeared, had her doubting everything. She slipped into one of the two chairs in front of his desk.

He surprised her by sitting in the other. "How is my wife doing?"

Oh boy, wasn't that a loaded question. Wait, last time she was here he'd already known. "I think she's doing very well, how do you think she's doing?"

He sat back. "How would I know? This is your case. Is something wrong?"

She stared him in the eye. "Cameron, you know exactly how your wife is."

"Maybe I do and maybe I don't. I'd like to hear your thoughts on the matter."

Oh, if that wasn't an evasive answer, nothing was. She wanted to ask him outright, but the plan was to be sweet. She pasted on a smile. "I think Holly is doing very well." She studied him, looking for a silver glow, but there was nothing. "She seems ready to get involved in town right after Christmas."

"So the visit with Ethan went well?"

She ignored the curious gleam in his eye. "Of course. She is just thrilled that Ethan is in love with someone. She said you despaired of that ever happening."

Cameron nodded. "That's true, I did. Who is Ethan in love with?"

Her gut screamed Cameron would know if she lied. "He didn't reveal it, but don't worry, Holly is determined to find out. I think our next visit will be the last. We're going to Brody's party. He invited her again this year."

Cameron nodded and looked away. "I know. That's why I chose you and Ian to get her to rejoin the living." He sat silent, staring at his desk as if it could send him back in time. Coco couldn't help but feel bad for him. He and Holly did have something special.

On the other hand, it shouldn't be at the expense of others. "Why did you assign this case to Ian? Why not just me? You said you needed my gift, which I've seen come into play a number of times. So why Ian?"

He started as if he'd been a million miles away. He probably was. "Why? Hasn't he been helpful?"

"That's not the point. Why did you want him on this case with me? You said when we started, Ian was the only one who could get the job done, which by the way is quite a slap in the face to the rest of us."

Cameron's face softened. "I didn't mean it that way. If you'll also remember I said it was as important to him as it is to me, though he doesn't know it yet."

His words triggered the memory. "Are you saying that I basically have two cases to handle, Holly's and Ian's?"

Her boss stood. "No, I don't expect you to handle Ian. He may be a lost cause. I'll deal with him."

Oh shoot, she didn't like the sound of that. "We aren't exactly done yet. Whatever you want from Ian may still materialize, though if you told me what it was, I might be able to help."

Cameron waved her off as he walked around to the chair at his desk. "It's not your responsibility. Just get my wife to see that not all is as it appears and I'll be happy."

His attitude about Ian, infuriated her. It was as if he'd written the man off. Sure, she wasn't happy with him and he was her supposed soulmate, but he had a lot going for him. He was very intelligent, kind to the living, and made her feel amazing when they had sex, though she doubted that was important to Cameron.

Maybe she could figure out her boss's purpose for Ian by digging a bit deeper about Holly. Despite Ian's warning, she needed to know.

Time to take the bull by the horns, in a nice way, of course. "Cameron, do you want Holly to discover who Ethan loves?"

He'd just sat down and his head snapped up to look at her. "What has that got to do with Ian?"

She shrugged. "Not much except that if you want her to find out, we could take a little detour before going to Brody's."

Cameron's eyes grew shrewd and for the first time, she completely believed what Ian said about him. The man would do anything for his wife, including rid himself of troublesome spirits. Her chest tightened and she found herself taking shallow breaths, her palms sweating in her lap.

"Why? Do you know who Ethan is in love with?"

She wanted to look away from Cameron's glittering hazel eyes, now almost green in their intensity. She swallowed. "I—"

"Yes, we know." Ian's voice behind her had her swiveling in her chair.

He strode forward and pulled her arm to make her stand. Seriously? The man could be such a Neanderthal sometimes.

"But we need to discuss our next visit. If you will excuse us."

Before she knew what was happening, Ian had phased her and dropped her in her apartment. She put her hands on her hips. "Making an enemy of our boss is not—"

Ian flew through her roof and was gone.

Ugh, the man was going to drive her crazy. But he also wouldn't get away from her that easily. There were only two places he'd go. Either back to have it out with Cameron or to his family home, and either way, she planned to find him and set him straight on a few issues he had.

As for her supposed soulmate connection, she would ignore it. This case hadn't been normal since the start and she couldn't trust anything at this point, except possibly Ian.

Shaking her head at that paradox, she flew into the ether.

Ian didn't stop once he left Coco at home. He knew better than to think she'd stay there, but he was certain she wouldn't be having another conversation with Cameron any time soon.

Even as he flew toward Glasgow, his gut tightened at how close he'd come to her telling Cameron about Holly's soulmate. It had taken him some time to realize what she might do. His punishment would only get worse if anything happened to Coco. Not because of what the higher-ups could do to him, but because knowing she was gone and he could have prevented it would kill him all over again.

He floated through the roof of his flat and into his living room. Solidifying, he strode to the kitchen and opened the trash cupboard to find it empty. Of course, everything was in its proper place in the afterlife.

"Make this flat exactly as it was the moment I discovered Ella's body."

Saying the words out loud left a bitter taste in his mouth, so he moved to the refrigerator to grab an ale, but there was only wine. That's right, he'd switched to drinking wine at home because it was what Ella preferred.

Taking out a bottle of Pinot Grigio, he poured himself a glass and gulped it down. Too bad he couldn't get drunk in the afterlife, but maybe the alcohol would make this easier.

He left the wine glass on the counter and forced his legs to move him toward the bedroom. Just outside the room, he stopped. He would prove to Coco his punishment was not of his own making.

Opening the door, he hesitated to enter. Ella lay across the bed, two empty pill bottles on the floor next to the hem of the tan quilt. The doctors said she'd mixed prescription medication with meth. Where had she'd bought it? How did she even know where to find it?

Probably one of her uni friends.

He ignored the empty pill bottles and went to her side of the bed. In the nightstand was another empty bottle, but it wasn't the medication she was supposed to take for her depression.

Striding into their bathroom, he had to believe she hadn't lied. Every day he asked her if she'd taken it because sometimes she forgot. When she said no, she always took it and thanked him for caring so much about her.

She took her own life at the end of December. All her medications were refilled at the start of the month, but she always refilled them a month in advance, more proof she wanted to be healthy.

He opened the top drawer next to her sink. There were no bottles in there. Opening the next one down, he stared in horror. It was filled with prescription bottles. Hesitantly, he lifted one. It was full, filled in October. He lifted another. It was filled in August. He didn't need to look at the rest. He could easily see they all had pills in them.

When did she stop taking them? Why had she lied to him?

He should have known. Why didn't he know? He did. He even commented to his mother that some months were better for Ella than others. He'd been too slow to understand.

He'd failed again.

"You couldn't have stopped her."

At the sound of Coco's voice, he spun around. He didn't want her here. How the fuck had she found him so quickly? "Of course I could have, if I'd been more observant. If I'd been the person she needed."

Coco looked over at the bed. "That's what you can't seem to get through that thick head of yours. No one could be the person she needed. That person would have to have superpowers. What she needed was impossible."

Coco's presence in the room dulled the tragedy somehow. He needed to get her out of there. He strode toward her, blocking her view of Ella. "It wasn't impossible."

"It was. What Ella needed was peace. She could only find that in death."

He brushed by Coco, determined to get her out of the room. "You don't know what you're talking about."

She followed him. "I know enough about her to know that if it wasn't you, it would have been someone else and she still would have taken those pills." Coco stepped in front of him as if she could physically make him see her point of view. "Believe it or not, as important as you think you are, you couldn't have made a difference in this outcome. If not that day, then another. If not you, then someone else. Nothing and no one could have kept her from seeking a release from life."

He fisted his hands. "I could have."

Coco slapped him across the face. The sting of her hand sent a shockwave through him.

"What's wrong with you? Are you afraid to admit you were powerless to stop Ella? Is that it? Because if you did that, then all this would have to stop. That's it, isn't it?"

He ignored the burn in his cheek. He deserved it and much more. "What would have to stop? What are you talking about?"

Coco stepped back, her eyes bright with understanding. "Your guilt. If you accept that there was nothing you could have done to prevent Ella from taking her own life, then you'd have to admit you were powerless and you'd have to stop punishing yourself."

Ian stared at her as if she'd sprouted wings. "You forget. I was the man she loved. I was the one who loved her."

She spread her arms wide. "Everyone loved her. Her parents, her brother, her professors. It didn't matter. Can't you see that? Ella had the best of everything. The best family, the best medical care, the best fiancé. She wasn't like the rest of us poor shmucks who have to struggle through life. Yet even with all that at her fingertips, and the love she was surrounded by, she was unhappy. It was chemical, Ian."

He'd never thought to compare what Coco had to what Ella

had. Why was Coco still so full of warmth even in the afterlife, yet Ella was cold even while living? "That's what her medication was for."

Coco shook her head. "Which she didn't take. *She* chose not to take it. *She* chose to end her life. No one could have changed that."

And that didn't make sense. "I'm done having this conversation."

Coco stared at him, the compassion in her gaze too much for him to take. He walked to the window and stared out at the empty bridge. He was well aware none of this was real. He wasn't even real, yet he existed. But Ella's death was real.

At the touch of Coco's hand on his back he looked over his shoulder. "What?"

"You don't need to punish yourself anymore. You're the only one here who blames *you* for Ella's death."

He snorted. "There are plenty of those still alive who blame me."

"Well, they're wrong."

He turned back toward the window, but the flicker of hope Coco started inside him when he brought her fulfillment grew stronger, trying to sway him to her way of thinking. He ignored it. "We need to bring Holly to her last visit."

"We need to tell Cameron about Holly's soulmate."

He turned at that. "No." He held his hand up as she opened her mouth. "Not yet. But yes, we will tell him."

Coco grinned. "We?"

He folded his arms. "Yes, we. I know if I don't agree to that you'll go behind my back."

She raised both eyebrows in a fake innocent look. "Maybe."

He shook his head and dropped his arms. "There's no maybe about it. Let's go."

"Wait. I have to change."

He took the opportunity to look at her from the t-shirt hugging her bountiful chest to the pair of jeans that were just a little too tight, making him want to get her out of them so she could breathe properly. "What's wrong with what you're wearing?"

She rolled her eyes. "We're going to a party. I need to change. I'll meet you back at Ethan's."

Before he could object, she floated through the floor and was gone.

The oppressive atmosphere of the flat immediately crowded in. "Change the flat to now." Interestingly, that seemed to help. "Add Christmas decorations and a tree."

Instantly, the flat turned festive. Not as festive as Holly's home, but definitely an improvement. It felt closer to how it was when Coco was in it.

He shook his head. Here he was scolding Holly for not celebrating Christmas when he didn't either. Then again, Holly wasn't guilty of anything. If anyone had guilt, it was Cameron.

Ian paused at that thought. If this would be his last assignment, which he grew more sure of with each passing action, he might as well go out in a blaze of glory. There were only three things he wanted to do before that happened, and if this was their last visit for Holly, he didn't have much time.

He smirked at the paradox. Who would have thought he'd be pressed for time in a timeless afterlife?

Coco flew into her apartment, solidified and went straight to her closet. Seeing Ian with a golden glow around him had her instincts pushing her to save him. The man was more stubborn than a lazy heifer.

Pushing aside her everyday wear, she went to the back and found what she'd been looking for. Carefully, she pulled the pink silky gown out, it's cellophane rustling as she moved it to a hook on her bedroom door.

She'd never worn it. She and Lynzie had gone shopping for the perfect New Year's party dresses, but she'd died before ever wearing it. It didn't exactly say Christmas, but it did say "party."

Her palms sweated as she pulled the plastic off. Wiping her hands on her jeans, she touched the silky, stretchy fabric. It hugged all her curves, hiding nothing, but what did she have left to hide? Ian had seen her naked body, so it wasn't as if this would be a surprise.

Quickly, she found the magazine page she had saved with the hairstyle she wanted. The updo only took the back of her hair into a knot high on her head while the long strands on either side were curled, which meant they bounced when she moved. She liked that.

Placing her hand against the dress, she had her nails colored to match. She'd never found the perfect shoes, so she requested strappy high heels to match. Lastly, she changed into the dress with a wave of her hand.

Hesitantly, she walked to the mirror in the bathroom.

"Wow." She studied herself, critically. Everything looked great except her big arms. She'd never gone without at least a half sleeve. Why had she bought spaghetti straps? Oh, she had planned to look for a gauzy shawl.

In the afterlife, she could just have her appearance changed. Thinner arms were possible within seconds. She stared hard before shaking her head. Then it wouldn't be her. Instead, she chose pink glitter for her hair and arms.

Now she was ready to impress her soulmate. Ever since coming back from Ian's Glasgow flat, she'd been thinking about the warm glow he had. The only people who knew she saw a glow were Ian, Holly, and Cameron if he'd been listening to them, which she had no doubt he had. But the chance that he could affect the same exact glow that she'd seen all her life was slim.

She was more convinced than ever that Ian was her soulmate. Her biggest obstacle was getting him to accept he'd had no culpability in Ella's death. Now that she'd found him, she really didn't want to lose him.

She smacked her forehead with her palm. The man was foreign and he was the first foreign spirit she'd ever worked with though not the first she'd met. Did that mean they were supposed to meet in the afterlife?

Her only hesitation was the timing. Why hadn't she seen the glow when they first met? Maybe the bigger question was, did it matter? The fact was, the arrogant man had grown on her, and her heart beat faster when she was around him. She was pretty sure she could fall in love with him if he would stop punishing himself for something he didn't do.

She took a deep breath and nodded at her reflection. "Okay, I'm as ready as I'll ever be." Phasing, she flew out her front window and to Ethan's.

When she arrived, Ian wasn't there. He should be any second though.

"Wow, look at you." Holly smiled. "You look amazing."

Coco flushed. "Thank you. Since you have my Christmas dress, I figured I could wear my New Year's dress for Brody's party."

Holly eyed her skeptically. "You do realize no one is going to see you, right. I mean, except myself and Ian." She wiggled her brows.

"Of course I know that. But as a spirit guide, it can get a little boring. It's not like I go to a Christmas party every day."

"You don't?" Holly's curiosity sparkled in her eyes. "Do you go to any parties? You are the Spirit of Christmas Present so I'd expect there must be some kind of festivities to attend. Do you ever see Cameron?"

Coco put up her hand. "Hold on there. I can't answer any of those questions."

Holly's smile left her face and she moved back to Ethan.

Coco couldn't help feeling sad for her. The woman had an amazing connection with Cameron, and they were suffering for it. How would she ever tell Cameron that Ethan was Holly's soulmate?

Holly's interest in Ethan's conversation with his mother, made Coco nervous. Maybe they should go to Brody's and have Ian meet them there.

She floated to where Holly hovered. Clearly, she was frustrated. "He stopped talking about the woman he's in love with. He isn't making this very easy."

Coco sighed with relief. "To be fair, it's not like he knows you're here."

Holly crossed her arms, reminding Coco of Ian.

Just then Ethan stood. "It's late enough. I better go straightaway." He took his wallet from his back pocket and reached inside. "Here's the painter Mr. MacDonald was asking about." Ethan pulled out a business card and dropped it on the table.

Coco sucked in her breath at the picture of Holly in the front of Ethan's wallet. She quickly floated between him and her charge. "I don't know what's keeping Ian. We can't go to Brody's until he gets here."

"Really? I thought he was a master at showing up on time. If you want, I can follow Ethan and you can find Ian." Holly's hopeful look was hard to resist, but Coco couldn't risk Holly finding out about Ethan, at least not without her present.

"No, I'll wait with you here until he arrives."

"Until who arrives?" Ian's voice behind her had her spinning, but one look at him in his family kilt left her breathless.

Chapter Ten

The green, red and white kilt Ian wore was covered at the top by a very formal black waist-length jacket with a waistcoat beneath. There were white ruffles at his wrists and neck. Below the kilt she could see his bare knees and his muscular calves were covered in tartan hose the same color as the kilt with a short green solid piece of material hanging from the top and what looked like a dagger tucked in the top on one leg. His shoes were black like the type someone might wear with a tuxedo.

The whole outfit hugged his waist, showing off his broad shoulders, and his red hair stood out even more with the black jacket. She tried to bring air into her lungs to fill the silence, but she still couldn't speak. Ian was truly spectacular.

She gazed into his eyes which had turned a dark gray. That color made her feel sexy and desirable.

"Oi, lass you aboot take my breath away." His voice lowered in tone sending shivers across her skin.

"Me?" Her word came out in a squeak. She swallowed and pulled more air into her lungs. "You are devastating. A girl could forget herself around you."

Holly giggled and they both looked at her.

"You two are dressed to the nines, but your colors clash something awful." She grinned. "I'd say that's par for the course."

Coco laughed, appreciating the point, but Ian frowned. She held her dress out a bit. "I could change, if you think we should—"

"No." Ian shook his head. "You're too bonny in that. We do not need to match." He glanced at Holly. "I match Holly perfectly thanks to your dress."

She didn't like that at all. But she did like the way he kept looking at her as if he couldn't believe what he was seeing. "I thought you don't get dressed for assignments."

He looked away. "I don't, but this one is special."

She wasn't sure if he meant because of her or Holly or something else, but right now she didn't care. The man was more than she'd ever imagined. She smiled. With so many clothes on his body, fitting him so well, it made her want to get them off him even more.

"Shall we?" Ian crooked both his arms.

She smiled at Holly. "We shall."

He floated them up through the roof and down the street.

"Ian, would it be acceptable for us to enter through the front door as if we were really going to a party?"

He looked down at her, his gaze so caring, she wanted to pinch herself to see if she was dreaming. Maybe it was just the reflection of his constant golden glow that had her misreading him. Or maybe she just saw what she wanted to see.

"Of course." He floated them down to the front of Brody's house. Cars were parked all along the street.

Holly pointed at the brick home. "This is his and Sarah's new house. Well, it's not a new house but it's new to them. Brody bought it this year. He said he wanted a house, not a flat to bring his bride home to. They're getting married this spring."

Coco smiled. It was a sweet thought. Could she and Ian have any kind of future, such as it was, in the afterlife? It would all hinge on him.

"After you, ladies." Ian let go of her hand, but rested his against the small of her back as if he were escorting her to a real party.

She felt cared for and had to take a sideways glance at him to be sure she wasn't imagining things. His strong profile was as harsh as always, but if she didn't know better, she'd think his lips had the slightest tilt upward.

Once inside, she expected chaos like at the parties they had in her local pub or at the brewery in town. At the very least, she expected it to be active like at Luca's, but the people were rather sedate at the moment.

Groups of three to five stood around chatting, most were about her and Holly's ages. No young children ran between parents' legs and no older parents needed tending to. But there were some older folks which was good because Mrs. Bell and Mr. Wrenford should be there somewhere.

"Look, there's Ethan. I wonder if he'll tell Sarah who his love is."

Before she could say anything, Ian clamped his hand down on Holly's shoulder. "I believe you were going to handle that task starting tomorrow. We are here to see Brody."

Holly's smile turned sad. "I was afraid you'd say that."

Coco was confused. "I thought you liked Brody."

"Oh, I do. It's just that while Ethan reminds me of the times we spent with Cam, Brody reminds me of Cam period. They were so alike, impetuous, adventurous, always living life to the fullest and throwing caution to the winds."

"It must be hard." Coco kept her focus on Holly's relationship with Cameron though it was difficult with her glowing golden again. "But I imagine Brody misses Cameron and being around you makes it feel like a piece of him is still here."

Holly shrugged. "I don't know. He has Sarah. His life has continued."

Coco cocked her head. "Last I checked, you were still living."

"True, but it doesn't feel like living."

Ian opened his mouth with what Coco felt sure would be a reprimand so she jumped in. "What would make it feel like living again?"

Holly snapped her gaze away from the party goers. "If I had Cam back."

"But besides that?"

Holly appeared to think on that.

Ian squeezed her hand. Coco looked up at him and he nodded, a small smile playing on his lips. Then he mouthed "Good question."

She wasn't sure if it was the smile or his praise, but her heart warmed for the man next to her. Maybe there was hope for him after all.

"I think for me to feel like I'm living I would need to care about something or someone. My only purpose now is the shop. Maybe if I could get my mom and John over here for a vacation or if I could track down Cam's sister and get to know her. I think I'd like that."

Ian opened his arm to indicate that they float into the next room. "Both of those goals are worthy."

Holly floated in front of them, so when she stopped suddenly, they had to release hands and float to either side of her. Was something wrong? Coco scanned the scene. More people were gathered in groups in the living room and a lovely tree filled the corner. "What is it Holly?"

Holly pointed, her eyes filling with tears.

It was a photo in a frame above the fireplace. Unlike the painting Ian kept above his, this one was a happy one. Brody and Sarah were at the center with Loudon Castle as the backdrop. Ethan was next to Sarah and Holly and Cameron were next to Brody. All had their arms around each other's waists and bore wide smiles.

Coco put her hand on Holly's arm. "That looks like a wonderful day." Holly nodded and sniffed. "It was. It was the day Brody proposed to Sarah. We were all thrilled for them."

Coco nudged Holly away from the picture. "It looks like they are still happy."

Brody had his arm around Sarah's waist and gave her side squeeze at that moment. She laughed, blushing.

Holly smiled, quick to move out of sadness, which was a good sign. "I always thought they were meant for each other. Wait a minute." She turned to Coco. "Are they soulmates?"

She grinned. "As a matter of fact, they are." Once again she felt the joy of sharing the soulmate knowledge with someone who was excited by it. She hadn't had that since she was alive.

But last time she and Holly got excited, Ian went into a funk. She glanced back at him. He wasn't frowning, and it looked like he still had that tiny uplift to his lips. Shoot, the man was hot in his formal wear.

"Coco, since you didn't find your soulmate while you were, um, alive. Is there still a chance you can find him?" Holly's question caught her off guard, and she turned to face her.

"Everything is different for me now, but I think I could."

Holly nodded toward Ian. "How about him?"

She laughed. "I think you should keep your matchmaking to the living and let me handle the spirit side, okay?"

"Okay." Holly scanned the room. "Are there any other soulmates here?"

She pretended to study the room, but the golden glows were easy to spot. They all had a slightly different color, so she did have to match them up. "I've seen at least three but the matches aren't all in this room."

"Oh, this is like a Christmas game." Holly hooked her arm in Coco's and turned them to face Ian. "We're going soulmate hunting. Want to come?"

He waved his hand to the side. "No. You two enjoy."

As Holly floated them past Ian, Coco couldn't resist blowing him a kiss.

When he raised that right brow of his, she laughed.

Ian enjoyed the view of Coco's back as she floated away. The bright pink dress had an open back that went all the way to her ass. He hadn't been able to resist touching her there as they floated up the walk.

Tonight, she was what his friends would call a "stunner." But she was so much more than that to him. She was hope.

Once the women disappeared from sight, he floated through the roof and flew into the ether. He landed in his study in no time. He looked at the painting above the fireplace and grinned. Coco, beautifully naked, still graced his room.

It was a huge improvement. That it hadn't disappeared told him his gut was right.

At the sight, he rearranged his plan of action. His investigation into Cameron could wait. Immediately, he flew through the roof and down to the very end of the west wing. At the end was the best guest room of the thirty his family home boasted, or at least in *his* opinion.

He solidified once in it and turned on the lights. Since he hadn't been in it since his first day in the afterlife when he explored his surroundings, it was just as it had been when he was alive.

The room was situated at end of the wing, not a turret per se, but a long curved wall with side-by-side fifteen-foot windows that looked out on the grounds and nearby tended forest. He opened a curtain and let in more natural light as far as the afterlife was concerned.

The four-poster bed sat in the center of the room, the foot of the bed facing the view. That would be a great sight in the morning. The bed was made up with silver sheets and the walls were grey with black trim to give it a modern-day look, despite the fact the wing had been built in 1874.

"Give the room forest green and pink décor with the bed in pink." Instantaneously, the room brightened, the pale pink was soft like Coco and the green was dark and hard like himself. It was far better than his own bedroom and the memories that one held.

He walked to the corner where a square sunken hot tub made of marble was placed. The marble was pink now as well. "Heat the tub." A light went on inside and steam rose. Perfect.

The décor matched Coco's soft side, but she had a very passionate side as well. He studied the room and came back to the hot tub. "Add floor to ceiling mirrors on the walls adjacent to the hot tub."

The walls turned to mirrors which reflected most of the room. He grinned. His gut said Coco would find that exciting. She wasn't skinny like most of his girlfriends had been, but he much preferred her hour glass shape. It drew him like no other body shape he'd ever been with.

He may not have time to have a real relationship with her, but if they only had one more time together, which was his guess, he wanted her to know how much he appreciated her.

Moving toward the bed, he noticed it was adjustable. He didn't always remember every detail of every room in the family home, especially because he had left as soon as he graduated university. The problem with an adjustable bed was the head and feet rose. For making love, he'd rather the center rose.

Making love? The thought made him pause. He didn't have the right to love another woman. He'd failed the last woman he loved so completely. But if he could save Coco from Cameron's wrath, maybe, just maybe he could be worthy of loving.

He snorted. It was a significant leap from enjoying sex to loving. To expect that Coco might actually feel like that about him was presumptuous on his part. But if as he expected, his existence in the afterlife would be ending soon, he'd give himself permission to presume. To hope.

Blinking, he moved his concentration back to the task at hand. "Make the bed adjust so the center raises and the head and foot move down." Not sure if that was possible, he picked up the control and tried it.

His lips quirked as the center of the bed rose. His cock agreed, growing hard as he imagined Coco's hips rising with the bed, her legs splayed wide. She would be beautiful. But would she realize that? He looked up at the ceiling above the bed. It was far above it.

"Top the bed with a well-mounted mirror that can stand a lot of shaking." A mirror appeared above the bed. Now Coco could see everything he saw and vice versa. He'd like to stay in this room with her for the equivalent of a living week.

Stepping back from the bed, he examined the room. It was a hundred percent better, but it was still missing something. It looked like a hotel room. It wasn't "homey" like Coco's place.

"A bucket of champagne next to the hot tub, strawberries and whipped cream next to the bed. A vase of red, white and pink roses on the breakfast table." As he made his wishes known, the items appeared. "A green afghan on the easy chair. Two robes, one for me and one for Coco over the headboard. Some magazines next to the flowers."

Now he could see bringing Coco here. They could enjoy each other one last time before he confronted Cameron. Pleased with his preparations, he phased and returned to his study. Turning his back on the alluring painting of Coco, he strode to his desk and sat.

He took a deep breath. His next step would change everything.

"Give me the file on Cameron Douglas."

Nothing appeared on his desk. He waited. He was actually overstepping his bounds, or so he'd been given to believe. If this didn't work, he'd have to do it the hard way and track down a Spirit of Christmas Past. None of whom liked him, he was sure.

A green file appeared on his desk and he let out the breath he'd been holding. It was a thick file considering Cameron was only about his age. That surprised him. Then again, he had only seen children's files and they tended to be very thin. Holly's didn't count since Cameron had obviously taken out most of the information.

Cameron would be alerted he'd requested the file, so he couldn't delay. The man could rescind it at any moment.

For the first time, he doubted his path, but it was Coco that had him hesitating and there was no certain future there, especially if he couldn't protect her. This was the only way.

With no more hesitation, Ian opened the file and Cameron's life began to play on the sheets before him like a movie.

"That's all of them." Coco smiled at Holly. "Do you think you'll remember them by time Christmas is over?"

Holly nodded. "It's too bad Mrs. Bell and Mr. Wrenford aren't soulmates, but I guess if they keep getting along so well, they can be good company for each other." She shrugged. "Three couples aren't that many to remember. Plus, I have to find out about Ethan, but for all we know he may not be in love with his soulmate, but I really hope he is. This is more complicated than I expected."

Coco took a deep breath, relieved that Holly hadn't asked her if Ethan's soulmate was at the party. Pointing out Mrs. Bell and Mr. Winfred's growing friendship had saved her. "What about all the other things you are planning to do. Do you remember them as well?"

"Of course. I have to call Mr. Branson, visit my family and convince Mom and John to take a vacation here, and track down my new sister-in-law. I wonder if Cameron's aunt knows about his half-sister."

"I don't know that."

Holly's face fell. I thought you spirits knew everything."

Coco chuckled. "No, we are very compartmentalized. Past, Present, and Future only know their specific area."

Holly floated toward the room with Sarah and Brody. Ethan joined them as champagne was being passed to everyone. "So I guess you can't tell me if Sarah will lose Brody early in their marriage."

Coco stared at Holly in surprise. "Why would you think that?"

Holly crossed her arms. "Because he's just like Cam. Always taking risks. Always trying new things, scary things. I'd hate for Sarah to experience what I've gone through."

Holly turned away from Brody and looked at Coco. "Sometimes I wake up in the morning and I don't want to get out of bed knowing that I won't see Cam. He became my world in so short a time and then in an instant he was gone. I felt like I hadn't lived before I met him. Now I feel like I'm going through the motions."

Coco wanted to say something that would comfort Holly, but the woman's sorrow was so profound, words failed her. Instead, she wrapped her arm around Holly's waist and gave her a squeeze.

Holly turned back to watch her three friends.

Was that all they had accomplished was to give Holly more "motions" that wouldn't engage her heart. Coco shifted her gaze to Ethan. If he was Holly's hope, maybe she needed to tell her. At least get her thinking about it.

Brody tapped his glass with Sarah's. "Quiet everyone. It's time for our Christmas Eve toast."

The room settled down and others filtered in from the other rooms, crowding the doorways when no more could fit.

"I'd like to propose a toast. To all our friends and family who are here and all those who could not come. To all the friends we have lost touch with and to those we have yet to make. A very Merry Christmas Eve. I wish you peace, happiness, and long life."

"Here! Here!" The response was heard around the room.

Ethan raised his glass. "And especially to our friend Holly Douglas, may she find peace and be with us next year!"

"To Holly!" As the chorus resounded, Coco's heart melted at the look in Ethan's eyes.

"Holy crap, I can't believe they toasted me. Me?" Holly's eyes filled with tears.

"Of course they did. Everyone here doesn't pity you, they miss you. You are a part of their lives whether you participate or not. They want you to be with them."

"I didn't realize this."

Sarah spoke to Ethan. "Thank you for that. I really hope she'll come next year."

"I'm going to invite her every year, no matter how many times she turns us down. She belongs with us." Brody's statement was heard by more than one person.

Someone yelled. "Let's go to her house and make her join us."

"Yes, let's go straightaway." Another voice chimed in.

Holly was crying buckets now.

Coco reached over and unpinned the Fergusson tartan from Holly's shoulder and handed it to her to wipe her face. "Here."

Holly nodded and covered her eyes with the material.

"Wait." Ethan's voice stopped what looked like could turn into a very real mob out to bring Holly back. "We cannot force her to be with us. Think of how miserable she would be. I have faith that she will join us eventually. None of us knows what it feels like to walk in her footsteps. Let her come to us when she's ready."

Brody patted Ethan on the back. "Always the sensible one, my friend. We will allow her to celebrate this year as she wishes, but I make no guarantees for next year." A number of people laughed, but Ethan frowned.

Holly managed to smile through her tears. "Dear Ethan. He

is so much more sensitive than Brody. I'm so glad he was Cam's friend."

Coco couldn't resist the opening. "He's your friend as well, isn't he?"

"Of course. These three people right here are my dearest friends."

"But you haven't spent any time with them in over a year, right?"

Holly's eyes widened. "Wow, it's really been that long? I guess I should do something about that right?"

"How about now?" Ian's voice coming from behind had them both spinning around.

Coco frowned, but she didn't say anything. This was a big decision on Holly's part.

Holly looked back at her friends and then at them. "I don't want to miss Cam's visit."

Ian glanced at the clock across the room. "As long as you're home by half past eleven, he can still visit. I doubt he can stay a full thirty minutes."

"Because he might turn into a ghost?"

Coco stared at Ian. "I thought you didn't know about spirits turning into ghosts."

His whole faced tightened. "I didn't until a little while ago. I'll explain later." He looked at Holly. "Yes, that's why he can't stay too long. He loves you that much."

Holly's face brightened. "I love him that much too."

"So would you like me to make you solid, so you can stay here for a little while? You are definitely dressed for the occasion."

She looked back at her friends again, twisting the Fergusson scarf in her hands.

Coco tugged at the tartan and Holly turned back, letting it go. Coco smiled softly. "I don't think you should go to the party wearing the Fergusson plaid."

"I wish I had the Douglas tartan with me." Holly sighed.

Coco chuckled. "Sweetie, everyone here knows who you are. You don't need that. Go. Be with your friends. You deserve this night."

Holly nodded. "Okay, I will. But you better make me solid outside."

Ian's lips moved upwards. "Good choice. Remember, anything you saw here, you don't know about."

Holly floated by him towards the door. "Unless I heard it from a little birdie." She winked just before disappearing outside.

Coco grabbed his arm. "I hope this is okay."

He grasped her hand on his arm. "It's definitely, okay."

Ian was acting very different since she and Holly went soulmate hunting. He was more confident in their actions. She couldn't wait to get him alone to find out why.

Holly waited for them, her feet already on the ground. "Now that I decided, I can't wait to get in there."

Coco smiled. "I'm so glad to hear that. But I'm also sad because we have to say goodbye now."

"That's right. I won't see you again."

"No, but it was wonderful getting to know you. Don't forget everything you wanted to do."

Holly shook her head. "I won't. I promise."

Coco floated to her and gave her a hug while she still could. When she let go, she had to wipe away a tear herself. Holly was a very special person. She wished with all her heart that Ethan and she would be given a chance, but she kept that to herself.

Ian stepped up. "I'm proud of you. This is a big step, but I know it's the right one."

"Thank you, Ian." Holly gave him a hug as well. "Try not to argue with Coco too much without me as an audience."

He stepped back. "I promise."

Holly sighed. "Cam sends me the best Christmas spirits ever."

Coco laughed. "I'll be sure and tell him that." She winked.

"Are you ready to join the party?" Ian raised his right eyebrow with his question.

Holly nodded. "Absolutely."

He touched her shoulder and Holly solidified. "Thank you both."

They watched Holly knock. When it opened, Sarah squealed and pulled Holly inside, closing the door on the night.

Coco sighed. A little sad and a little worried. It was always hard leaving a case, but knowing what she knew made this one harder.

Ian's arm came around her and pulled her against his side. "She'll be fine."

She looked up at him. "I hope so. I know she's headed in the right direction, but I'm worried about Cameron standing in her way."

Ian's gaze turned hard at the mention of their boss. "He better not."

She couldn't help it. She turned to face him and touched his cheek. "Please don't say that like that. It makes me nervous."

His gaze softened as he lowered it to stare into her eyes. His arms wrapped around her and he pulled her close. "I think we need to celebrate our success."

She lifted her right brow. "Seriously?"

He smiled. "Seriously."

It wasn't just a tiny smile he gave her. It was a full-on, breath-stopping, knee-weakening smile and her heart opened. Whatever had shifted for Ian was big.

"You can close your mouth now, unless you're waiting for a kiss?"

Now he was teasing her? It was so out of character, she wasn't sure how to react, so she snapped her mouth closed.

Or did he mean it? She opened her mouth again and a shiver floated over her skin as Ian's eyes darkened.

"If it's a kiss you be wantin', a kiss you shall have." Ian lowered his face and his lips brushed her own lightly before he pulled back to gaze into her eyes. "I want you, Coco. No, I need you, more than my next breath. Come home with me?"

Her toes curled in her strappy high heels even as her heart lurched. "Yes."

Relief shone clearly in Ian's eyes, and she grasped his arms tighter.

How long had he kept himself an outsider with no one to talk to, eat with, touch? "Let's go celebrate."

He pulled her up against him and his mouth came down on hers. This kiss wasn't gentle, but it wasn't rough either. It was perfect, and as she closed her eyes, she tangled her tongue with his while he swept them through space and time to his home. When he pulled away and she opened her eyes, she didn't recognize where they were.

"Uh, Ian. I think you made a wrong turn."

He chuckled, sending warmth throughout her body. She could grow addicted to that sound.

"We are in the hallway of the west wing of my family home."

She looked around her, still anchored against him. It looked a bit dreary, but she didn't want to say anything negative.

"I have a surprise for you."

She cocked her head. "You scooted away during Brody's party, didn't you?"

His eyebrow rose. "You noticed?"

She rolled her eyes. "I noticed that you didn't find us for a while and when you did, you'd changed. I want to know what you were doing."

His grin was back and she had to take a steadying breath. Between the man, the clothes, and the smile, she was putty in his hands.

But he stepped away from her and solidified. "I'm about to show you."

She quickly solidified as well and turned toward the door he pointed at.

"Go ahead. Open it."

Chapter Eleven

Ian being mysterious and angry was the norm, so this new mischievous Ian took a little longer to trust. Even so, she turned the knob and opened the door. "Oh wow, this is amazing."

It was more than amazing. The room was perfect. She scanned the room from the breakfast table with flowers to the robes on the bed to the amazing view to the hot tub in the corner. She blushed as she could tell by the mirror that caught her looking at herself.

In the reflection, she could see Ian's full-blown smile complemented by his soulmate glow. There was so much more to him than what he'd shown everyone. But it was more than that. He'd changed. "Did you do all this for me?"

He nodded as he embraced her from behind. "Aye, I wanted it to reflect all the facets of you."

Oh boy, the man was burrowing deep into her heart with every word and action now. "She cocked her head. I'd say reflection is the right word."

He lowered his lips to the side of her exposed neck. "I want to see every flush and breath you take as I make love to you. Your passion draws me like a moth to a flame, but I don't fear being burned because it is your very warmth that gives me hope."

No one had spoken such beautiful words to her. That he had hope was far more than she'd ever expected of him. She watched in the mirror as his lips traced the side of her neck. Her bright pink silk against his dark black jacket and green plaid. Their dress couldn't be more opposite, yet they were meant to be together for eternity.

That knowledge almost buckled her knees, and she lifted her arms up to hold his neck. In the mirror, it looked as if she offered herself to him, which was exactly what she felt.

Ian's gentle touch changed at her surrender and his lips found his favorite place on her neck and he sucked. She arched at the possessiveness in his action.

His arm which had been wrapped around her waist loosened and he brought both hands up over her tummy to cup her breasts and squeeze them gently.

He lifted his lips from her neck and stared at her in the reflection. "I love your body. These curves," he lifted her breasts, "beckon me to touch them." He moved his thumbs to brush them against her hardening nipples, the silk material rasping against her skin.

Heat built between her thighs at his touch. His hands were so large and masculine against her body.

He moved them away from her breasts to press her pelvis back against him. At first all she felt was his sporran, but then that accoutrement disappeared and the hard ridge of his cock dug into the small off her back where her bare skin met the kilt.

She dropped her arms and held his wrists as she looked at him in the mirror. "I want to see all of you this time."

His lips quirked up. "I may need some help with that."

She stepped away and faced him. "Believe me, it will be my pleasure." At his knowing grin, she laughed. All the joy she felt at finding soulmates couldn't compare to what she experienced now. To be with her own soulmate. To have found him after all and to actually love him.

As she admitted her feelings, she felt a bond stronger than

anything she'd experienced, but she also could tell he wasn't there yet. Hmm, she may just have to convince him he loved her.

She started with the column of buttons down the center of his large chest, from the middle down and then up under the white ruffle. She could easily simply make it vanish, but the anticipation of unveiling him a piece at a time was too exciting.

Once she had that coat off him, there was a doublet and the ruffle about his neck. As she started to unbutton the formal white shirt beneath, Ian caught her hands. "Do ye have anthin' against tattoos?"

His Scottish accent always distracted her, so it took her a second to refocus on his question. "You have a tattoo?"

He nodded, his eyes uncertain.

Shoot, the man was full of surprises. He had such a straight-as-an-arrow bearing with his short red hair, broad shoulders, and perfect posture, that it never occurred to her he would have a tattoo. "She looked him square in the eyes. "I think tattoos are hot."

He chuckled as he lifted his hand to stroke her hair where the pink ran through it. "And I think pink streaks are 'hot'."

She was so used to having it that she often forgot it was there. "That may be, but you've already seen my pink streak. It's only fair I see your tattoo."

Despite their intimate position, he still seemed uncertain, which just made her more curious. Pushing aside the unbuttoned shirt she stilled.

Over his left pectoral was a large cross with an old world look to it. Instinct had her placing her hand on top of it and she could feel his heartbeat beneath her palm. She looked into his eyes. "It's beautiful."

He lifted her hand from his chest and brought it to his mouth and kissed it. "You're beautiful."

She didn't think she could ever tire of hearing him say that.

He laid her palm against his cheek. The action made her think of someone seeking warmth, asking to be invited in. He didn't realize he already was. She placed her other hand on his cross. "Tell me about it."

He gave her a lopsided smirk. "I wish I could tell you I had a religious epiphany of some kind or that I thought about being a minister."

She widened her eyes. "Oh, please don't tell me that."

His smile evened out again, showing his true warmth. "To be honest, I had it done to piss off my father."

"Seriously?"

"Seriously. He was so focused on making money and as a teenager I didn't know what I wanted to do with my life, but I knew I didn't want to be a slave to wealth. My dad not only disliked tattoos, but he disliked charity as well. Therefore, I had to get a tattoo of a cross." His lips quirked up. "I did it to be rebellious, but it's been a comfort at times."

Considering they existed in some kind of afterlife, she could see why that would be. She liked the idea that he would find comfort in it. Being raised in Kentucky, religion was a given, but this tattoo seemed to transcend even that for him. "I love it." She leaned forward and kissed it.

Ian's intake of breath reminded her that she hadn't had a chance to see him or touch him last time they were together. She didn't stop with his cross. She kissed a path over the two mounds that were his chest. Really, the man was all muscle.

She pulled back. "For an arrogant, wealthy man who didn't need to work, how come you have such a ripped body?" She ran her hand over the washboard stomach she'd never seen before. "I mean these are the real deal."

Ian's stomach tensed beneath her touch and when she looked up at him, he appeared to be blushing. Blushing?

"I had a personal trainer and a workout room in my flat. There's one here at the family home as well."

She didn't hide her admiration, staring at his hard torso. "Well, the money may buy you the equipment and the trainer, but it takes willpower to keep at it and I can tell, you definitely did that." She met his gaze. "But I never doubted your will."

"Ach, you be teasing me now. Be careful or this wilna go slow."

Between his words and his accent, she had to grasp his arm to keep her knees from buckling. Oh boy, the man could melt her with his words alone. Then again, she'd never had a man who wanted her like he did. It did wonders for ridding herself of all her body doubts.

She wiggled her brow at him. "Is it true what they say about what a Scotsman wears under his kilt?"

Ian laughed, his heart lighter than it had been since Ella died. Maybe he shouldn't think of her right now when another was in his arms, but it felt right. Not even the thought of his father's disapproving stare could dampen the feelings growing inside him.

He raised his right eyebrow. "That depends. What do they say?"

Coco cocked her head and smiled up at him. "That you don't wear anything under the kilt, but I just can't believe that. I think I need to verify."

Before he could stop her, she'd knelt at his feet and lifted his kilt. The cool air did nothing to mitigate his erection, but as her hand touched him, he grabbed her wrist. "Nay, you're not going to make me take you straightaway. I want to savor you like fine single malt Scotch.

"Since you put it that way." She grinned as she rose to stand before him again. "But you need to know that I've wanted to touch every inch of your skin since you took me in the ice cream shop."

At her words, his cock jumped beneath his kilt. The pleasure that episode had given him rushed through his body now, and he sucked in his breath.

Coco tugged on the leather strap that held his kilt on. He reached down to help her, and she slapped his hand. "No. I want to do it."

He smirked and dropped his hands to the sides. However, he did suck in his stomach which made it far easier for her to undo the leather straps.

"There." She smiled as the front of the kilt fell away only to stop where the inside strap held it about his waist. "I guess I'm really going to work for this." Determinedly, she unbelted the last strap and the kilt fell to the floor.

Coco stood back, her silky pink dress hugging every inch of her body. The hardness of her nipples strained against the fabric, calling for him to touch her. It took all his control not to reach out and pulled her toward him. Last time she'd let him have his way. To be fair, he needed to let her have her way for as long as he could.

"Wow. I knew you were hard, but someone should seriously create a sculpture of you."

He shook his head. "There are much better statues already in existence."

"I don't think so."

At her appreciative stare, he kept silent. Every area of skin she looked at felt as if it came alive beneath her gaze.

She walked around him. "Holy frick, you're as built on the backside as you are on the front. Do you have any fat on your body at all?"

"I'm sure I do."

"I don't know." At the touch of her hand on his back, need flew through him and settled in his groin.

Her hand traveled across his shoulders and he closed his eyes. It had been so long since he'd been touched by another. His physical form rejoiced as her hand travelled down to his ass and over it. When both her hands touched each side of his left thigh, he fisted his hands and forced himself to stay still.

She ran them down his thigh, past his knee and to the tartan hose he wore. Slowly, she worked the tall sock down. "Lift your foot."

He did as directed, and she pulled off his shoe and sock.

Then her hands went to his right thigh and she ran her hands down to the knee but stopped when she reached his sgian-dubh. "What's this?" She pulled the dirk from his sock slowly, sensitizing his skin even more. "That's a sgian-dubh and is part of Scottish formal dress."

"I guess that could come in handy if you were mugged."

He smiled at her comment, but the second her hands returned to his sock and pulled it down, he gritted his teeth to keep himself from yanking her up and throwing her on the bed.

When she'd finished undressing him, she walked around him one full time before stopping in front of him. She lifted her gaze from his body to look into his eyes. "Wow."

Her eyes had darkened to the color of honey and he could smell the chocolaty scent she exuded. In the mirror behind her, the low back of her dress tempted him with the top of her ass, while the front of her dress revealed how aroused she was.

That's all he needed to know because he couldn't keep his hands from her one more minute. He stepped up to her and pulled her against him. The silky feel of the pink material was arousing, but not as much as the curves beneath it.

"I think you have too many clothes on."

Before she could reply, he lowered his head and kissed her. This time he gentled his impulses somewhat and explored her mouth instead of ravishing it. He tasted some kind of mint on her tongue and wished it gone, her own flavor far more enticing.

Coco's arms wrapped around his neck and she pressed herself closer. A small whimper came from the back of her throat. It was too much. He wasn't made of stone, no matter what she thought he looked like.

Bending his knees, he swept her up into his arms.

She broke away from his lips. "Ack! Ian, what are you doing?"

He didn't answer, instead he took the three strides to the hot tub and without hesitation he walked down the steps into the warm water and sat with her in his lap.

"Oh no, my dress."

The material that already hugged her to perfection, soaked in every drop of water and clung to her like a second skin. He brushed her hair back from her face and rubbed the pink strands between his fingers. "You can make it as right as rain again. Dinna worry aboot it."

She kissed him on the chin. "You're right. I forgot. Maybe this could be a new look for me." She wiggled off his lap, only to cause his cock to harden more at her movements. When she was off, she crouched in the water to her neck then stood up and held her hands out to the side. "What do you think? A new fashion statement?"

Ian forgot to breath as he gazed at the pink material plastered to Coco like a second skin, not only showing off her hard nipples but the substantial curves of her breasts, the indent of her waist, the curve of her hips and the dark pubic hair nestled at the apex of her thighs.

"What?" She turned around to face the mirror. "Oh."

The weight of the water on the dress had caused the open back to dip lower and the top of the crease of her ass was visible above the water. He stepped up behind her and wrapped one arm around her waist, fitting his cock against the small of her back, and pinning one arm to her side.

With his other hand, he grasped one whole breast and kneaded.

Coco's head fell back against his shoulder, but she didn't close her eyes. Instead, she watched.

Triumph, pure and simple, filled his veins. He knew this woman. Releasing her breast, he flicked his fingers across her nipples, causing them to strain harder against the material. His arm about her waist tightened of its own accord, pressing her harder against him.

Then he smoothed his hand over her belly and to the dark spot outlined by the dress. He crinkled the dress up, pulling more and more wet material into his hand until he could reach his hand underneath.

He glanced at Coco to see her gaze riveted to his hand. He wouldn't disappoint her. Tucking the dress beneath his other arm, he splayed his hand over her mons. "Do you like the feel of my fingers inside you, lass?"

She nodded, her gaze still intense.

If he dove inside her amazing warmth, it wouldn't be long before he took her, but he couldn't deny her. Slowly, he moved two of his fingers between her thighs, coaxing her to open her legs wider. When he had clear access, he moved to her opening where silky wetness coated his fingers.

He swore he could smell her sweet scent rising with the steam of the water below. He wanted that scent around him. But he held off and coated his fingers with her own moisture before bringing it to cover her clit.

"Yes." Coco's breathless whisper was like a command. He moved his two fingers back to her opening and slid them inside. When they were as far as they could go, he moved his thumb to play against her clit.

Coco's pelvis pushed forward, giving him an even better view of his playground. He focused on her hard nub and the breaths she took as her excitement mounted.

He lowered his lips to her ear. "Come for me, lass."

"But I want you." Her voice was barely a whisper.

He kissed her ear. "I promise to dive inside you as soon as you reach your pleasure."

"But—"

He took her earlobe between his teeth and bit.

"Oh, oh." Coco's pants took over her words.

He ground his cock into the top of her ass even as his thumb kept a steady rhythm against her clit. He left his fingers buried inside her. He wanted to feel her pulse as she found her ecstasy.

She was close, reaching. He could feel her sheath contract as she climbed towards her pinnacle. He moved his hand from her waist and reached up and pushed it beneath the wet dress to grasp her breast.

Coco's whimper turned to a shout as she bucked against his hand. His fingers were coated by her juices. He held her close as her body shattered around him. He wanted to wait, let her recoup, but his need to be inside her wouldn't be denied.

Pulling his fingers from her opening, he brought them to his mouth and sucked. Her taste was ambrosia and his body flooded with energy.

Her eyes opened in time to see him take his fingers from his mouth and her moan heated him beyond his control.

"I canna wait." He pulled the spaghetti straps of her wet dress down until it bared her breasts.

The areolas were pebbled with her arousal, the tips peaked hard, despite her satisfaction. He bent her over and she grasped the side of the hot tub with her hands. Her lovely breasts swayed free, the mirror giving him the perfect view.

He caught her gaze in the reflection. "Now."

Her eyes widened even as they darkened with her desire. He'd already bent his knees and positioned his cock at the slick opening of her sheath. It was too much temptation. Quickly, he glanced at their reflection as he grasped her hips and plunged in.

"Yessss."

Coco's hiss gave him the permission he needed and he pulled back out only to thrust in again, watching her body flush with pleasure. He began a hard rhythm, pumping in and out with even strokes, savoring every sensation as his cock was sucked at by her sheath.

His balls tightened, but he refused to come without her. He brushed his palm across her swinging nipples as they moved back and forth. Whimpers started again in the back of her throat.

He smoothed his hands down her belly until he found her clit again and let his finger play there as he thrust.

Coco's noises grew louder even as his tension built. Grasping one of her shoulders, his other hand still at her clit, he held her in position as he rocked into her, thrusting deep, deeper, until his seed burst from him in a torrent of pleasure.

Coco's sheathe tightened around him, sucking all he had as she screamed her own delight. Heat flooded through him into her as if all that was bad was incinerated leaving him floating on air, purified, clean, and forever connected to her.

Even as the thought formed, he knew it was an illusion, but still he reveled in the possibility and bent over her, grasping her to him, never wanting to let her go.

As her arms gave way, he pulled her back with him and sank into the hot water, their bodies and souls still attached. He felt complete—happy.

"Wow." Coco looked at him in the mirror. "I've never, I mean that was—did you feel that bond?"

He had. It was celestial and strong, and he both clung to it and feared it. He lowered his head to kiss her shoulder and spoke against her skin, even as one hand came up to cup her breast. "I felt a lot of things."

She chuckled, the sound seeping into him as well. "You and me both. But I still didn't get to touch you." She pouted at him in the reflection.

He leaned her to the side so he could look her in the eyes. "If you had touched me any more, we wouldn't have made it into the tub."

Her breath caught at his words.

Happiness flowed through him that he could affect her so thoroughly. "But I promise you, you can have your way with my body soon."

She wiggled her brows. "I'm going to hold you to that."

He had no idea what Cameron's initial plan was in pairing the two of them up, but he would be eternally grateful to the man, despite all he'd learned about him. He just wished he had eternity to enjoy Coco.

"I don't think I need this anymore." She waved her hand and the bright pink dress that had been scrunched around her waist disappeared.

He couldn't resist the one piece of bare skin he hadn't touched yet and stroked across her tummy. "I love the feel of your skin."

"I love the feel of your mouth." She smiled enticingly, daring him to pleasure her again.

That was a dare he was willing to take. "Then I suggest we dry off and move to the bed."

She giggled. "I guarantee you, I'll still be wet."

That she referred to her delectable pussy wasn't lost on him or his cock, which still nestled inside her. It jumped to attention and she squeezed him.

He grasped her head in his hand and kissed her with all the passion he felt for her. She'd been his hope and now she was his salvation. He could never show her how much she truly meant to him.

As their tongues tangled, he moved his other hand up to tweak her nipple.

She broke the kiss. "Oh boy. If you're going to start that, we better leave this water before I get all wrinkly."

He smiled. "Then I could lick all those wrinkles."

Before he guessed what she would do, she stood, separating them, making him feel uncertain again.

"You make me hot enough as it is."

Despite the loss of her warmth, he remained where he was enjoying the sight of her in her naked glory. He'd love to show her the portrait in his study now.

"Come on." She pulled his hand. "You, too. Stand up for me so I can see the water roll down those awesome abs of yours."

Even at her words, his stomach muscles tensed. Happy to do as she wished, he rose slowly, loving the way her eyes rounded and she licked her lips as she stared at his body. His cock was already hard again and her gaze got stuck there.

He reached his hand out to lift her chin, but she suddenly dropped back into the water and grasped his erection with both hands.

"I'm sorry but I have to taste you."

Her mouth closed over his tip and it was all he could do to remain standing. She nibbled at his sensitive head before she pulled as much of him into her mouth as she could.

He grasped her head, wanting to encourage her and yet, wanting to stop her.

She pulled her head back then took him into her mouth again and sucked. His hand fisted her hair as his eyes closed. When she released him again, he took a steadying breath and opened his eyes.

In the mirror was the erotic tableau of her head sliding closer as she took him in her mouth again, the tips of her hair wet as they lay on her upper back and her rounded ass in the water tensing with her movements.

It was far too much for a man who hadn't been touched for so long. He fisted her hair in his hands, the pink streak firmly between his fingers and slowly pulled his hips away.

Coco looked up. "Can't I taste you?"

He didn't say anything, her words adding to his sexual need.

"Ian?"

"I canna. Not yet. I'll hurt you."

Coco cocked her head. "I'm not that fragile."

He loosened his hold on her head and grasped her shoulders to help her stand, the water sluicing down her body another enticement to taste her. He forced himself to be gentle and cupped her face. "It's been a long time. Be patient. Please?"

Her face softened and she covered his hands with hers. "Okay. For you."

He brushed her lips with the softest of kisses, knowing there would be no softness left in him. He wasn't simply starved for human touch, but he was addicted to Coco and his body, mind and soul wanted to gorge.

Bending, he swept her up in his arms again and brought her to the bed.

"Ian, I'm still wet."

He stood with her next to the bed. "I thought you'd be wet even if you were dried off."

She crinkled up her nose. "That's true."

He grinned. "Then I'll just have to dry you off." He lowered her to the bed and followed her down. The feel of her wet, curves beneath him was too much and he took her mouth with his.

Coco felt the second Ian lost his control. Something sparked from him to her as they touched full length and she parted her lips to catch her breath just as his tongue swept inside.

She'd been honest when she said she wasn't fragile and she proved it as his tongue swept into her mouth, dominating her with its explorations. She didn't pull back. Instead, she urged him on, moaning low in her throat as she grasped his head to her. She brought her leg over his, opening as best she could, inviting him to take what he needed.

The feel of the muscles on his back moving as his lips plundered her own revved her need up another notch. When he broke off the kiss, she turned her neck, knowing what he wanted. He groaned before his mouth latched onto her neck and he sucked, sending pleasure straight down to her core.

She reached down and grabbed his ass, pressing herself as close as she could get to him, encouraging him to move between her legs.

He let go of her neck and as promised began to lick at every drop on her body, though many had already dried in the heat they had created. He moved across her breasts, licking at droplets before circling each areola and sucking her nipples hard.

She arched off the bed as the sensations pinged to her pussy, readying it once more for his entrance.

Ian made his way down her body methodically, licking every bit of moisture including the drops in her pubic hair. When he brushed it aside to lick at her clit, she arched her pelvis up.

He lifted his head. "Give me that control." He pointed to what looked like a square remote. She handed it to him and he pressed it.

The bed rose in the center, lifting her hips six inches higher before he stopped it. Then without another word, his mouth descended on her folds and he lapped them before his large, strong tongue delved inside her.

Coco grabbed at the silken sheets as stars danced before her eyes. Ian held her thighs apart as he ate her like a man starved, lapping at her folds, spearing her opening, sucking on her clit until she thought she would explode.

He stopped suddenly, his dark gaze clear as he looked in her eyes from between her legs. "I need you again and again and again."

Her heart leapt, not at his words but at the look in his eyes as if he loved her and would do anything for her.

"She reached her hand down and fingered the short red hair at his temple. "Take me."

Ian rose on his knees and pulled her hips closer. Then he fell forward, his hands on either side of her. "Now?"

She nodded, her throat too tight to speak.

His dark gaze locked with hers and he thrust inside her. Sparks exploded between them, their glows like sparklers. He came down on his elbows and cradled her head in his hands.

She wrapped her legs and arms around him, needing him even closer than he was.

His mouth found hers and his tongue held hers as his hips pulled back and slammed home.

Joy splintered through her at his movement. His need for her, his strength and his heart all melted her and she allowed him to take her where he would.

"More —closer." Ian's rasped words penetrated her thoughts and she understood.

"Yes."

At her word, he phased into her solid body setting off her orgasm and sending them into a billion pieces. Her solid form kept them anchored as their souls entwined in ecstasy.

Ian floated out of her, solidified and drove his cock deep inside her one more time.

She grasped him to her, panting, unsure what had happened, but feeling that it was good.

After they both could breathe again, he lifted his head to look at her. "Thank you."

She gave him a soft smile. "Thank you. Your instinct was right. We had to do that." Then she winked. "And it was out of this world."

He chuckled, vibrating her breasts where his chest touched

them. His fingers found her pink streak and played. "I promise you, I will never fail you."

She grasped his hand in her own. "I know you won't. You've never failed anyone. It's just not in your nature."

He looked away and her gut tightened. As much as she didn't want to ruin their first real time together, he needed to know. "Ian, it's time to let go of the guilt. It doesn't belong to you."

"I disagree. There had to be something I could have done."

She turned his head to look at her. "You told Holly that if Cam ignored Ethan's advice on a regular basis, then Ethan's presence wouldn't have changed the outcome."

His brow furrowed. "Yes. That's true."

She barely stopped herself from rolling her eyes. "That means that if Ella didn't want to take her medicine and preferred to escape life, your presence, knowledge, or love still wouldn't have changed anything."

He stared at her blankly at first and then his eyes lightened. The lines around his eyes faded and his whole face softened. "I thought—"

She placed her finger over his lips. "Don't think. Feel. Feel it in your gut."

He raised his right eyebrow and she laughed. Then he sucked her finger into his mouth and her whole body came alive again.

Coco lay with her head upon Ian's chest. His heart beat was so strong beneath her ear, yet they existed in the afterlife and weren't technically "living." It was strange but wonderful.

She hadn't known what to expect after she died, but it definitely hadn't been the awesome experience she had. From being a spirit guide to finding Ian, it was far beyond anything she could have imagined. She lifted her head so she could look into his smoky gray eyes. "How did you die?"

He raised his right brow. "That is a rather personal question."

She rolled her eyes. "Considering what we've just done…and done, I think I'm entitled to a few personal questions."

"You are." He nodded at the same time his hand came up to stroke her hip. "I was in a plane crash."

She shivered. "That sounds awful."

"More awful than being hit by a car?"

She shrugged. "That only hurt for a short time. Besides, in my case I had control. *I* decided to push my friend out of the way, knowing I might not make it."

"And mine didn't hurt at all. I was actually coming to America. First, I visited a friend in Greenland. Then I took a small plane to America. I had planned to look at a small horse farm in Kentucky."

"Kentucky?"

"Yes. I'd decided to live abroad for a while and a horse farm in America seemed far enough from my past failures. But on the way out of Greenland, we flew into a snowstorm. I believe we hit the side of a mountain, but there was so little visibility, we could very well have crashed on the ground. It doesn't matter because either way I'm here now."

Coco's mind spun. "Lynzie's soulmate was in the process of selling a horse farm. I wonder if we were supposed to meet then, but then I saved her and messed everything up."

"What are you talking about?"

She looked away, but he turned her head to face him. "Don't keep anything from me. Please."

At his look, she swallowed. Ella had kept a lot from him and in essence he'd been left out. That he wanted to be inside with her, made her happy. It was nerve-racking though, not knowing how strong his feelings were for her. "I will never keep anything from you, unless it's a present or something good that is supposed to be a surprise."

"Coco." There was that scolding tone that she hated so much when she first started working with him, and now it just made her smile.

"Ian." She used the same tone, but ruined the effect by laughing.

"Please, tell me." His tone had softened and the insecurity in his gaze melted her heart.

"As you know, I had a feeling when I was alive that my soulmate was foreign. If I remember correctly, you accused me of doing nothing with that knowledge."

"I apologize. I should not have said that."

"Apology accepted. You weren't very happy at the time. But I wonder if you were the foreign man I was supposed to meet. You were flying to Kentucky and I lived there. I bet it was fate."

He shook his head and smiled sadly. "I guess we'll never know."

She took a deep breath. It was now or never. "But I do know. You're my soulmate. You and I have a golden glow."

Ian's eyes widened. "But how?"

"I don't know. There was no glow when I first met you or even after we started to work together, but it's there now."

"So you can see spirit soulmates, too?"

She shook her head. "No, that's the thing, and why I didn't trust it at first. It didn't appear to me until we had that argument in my apartment."

Ian looked away and her heart sank. "Are you upset you're my soulmate?" Though she tried to keep the shaking out of her voice, she failed.

His gaze swept back to her and he cupped her face in his hands. His own eyes were strangely moist. "Upset? I'm elated. I couldn't think of anyone else I could possibly have such a strong connection with. It explains why I couldn't resist you, no matter how hard I tried."

He brushed her hair back, his one hand fingering her pink locks. "Coco, I love you."

Her heart burst with joy and tears of happiness flooded her eyes. "I can't believe it! I mean, I do believe it, but—oh shoot, I love you too."

Ian brought his face to hers and kissed her. It was gentle and loving and filled her soul with peace. She lifted her lips from his to kiss his cheeks and chin, before leveraging herself up to gaze at him. The idea of going through the afterlife with him filled her with energy. "I can't wait to spend the rest of eternity with you. What should we do first?"

His smile faded. "I'm not sure that will be possible."

"Oh, for Pete's sake, Ian. Can't you stay happy for more than a minute at a time."

He raised his right brow. "I think I have been sufficiently happy for a number of hours, wouldn't you agree?"

She rolled her eyes. "Sufficiently? You always use your big words when you're hiding something serious. Oh." From the look on his face, she'd guessed right. "What is it?"

"I may have put our future in jeopardy."

Her stomach tightened. Ian wasn't playing around. "You did more than simply set up this room for me while I was with Holly at Brody's party, didn't you?"

He nodded, his eyes silver grey and growing harder by the second.

"What did you do, Ian?" She knelt next to him, bracing for the worst, ready to figure out how to fix whatever it was.

He took her hand in his and examined it. "I needed to protect you. The only way to do that was to understand what motivated Cameron."

"Oh no. What did you do?"

He finally met her gaze. "I pulled his file."

"Pulled his file? What file? Oh. Oh, you didn't!" Her stomach rolled over and threatened to come up on her. She pulled her hand from his and grasped her belly. Cameron would not let *that* go without punishment, no matter what Joy said about the afterlife. "You can't review a supervisor's life! What were you thinking?"

Chapter Twelve

Ian looked away. Despite her leg touching the side of his waist, he distanced himself mentally. Coco could feel it.

"I had to. I had to know why Cameron had us helping his wife and what power he had that could be a threat to us."

Despite her anxiety, her curiosity couldn't let it go. "What did you find out?"

He looked at her and shook his head. "I can't tell you. If I keep it to myself, then he can only be angry with me."

She stared at him with widened eyes. "Seriously?" She waved her hand between them. "This is a soulmate bond. There is no breaking this. You can't separate you from me anymore."

His whole body tensed next to her and he sat up, grabbing her arms. "We have to be separate. I can't let anything happen to you."

Her heart raced at the fear in his eyes. What did he know? Why was he so afraid for her?

"Coco, you are my only hope. Even if I face extinction, I can do it knowing you still thrive."

"Thrive? I won't thrive. I'd be like Holly." Oh boy, didn't that put things in a new light. "I've finally found you, and there's no way I'll let you go."

Ian's hands bit into her arms. "You may have to."

They were getting nowhere fast. "Okay, okay, let's look at this from a different angle. You're assuming that Cameron will be so angry that he won't let you continue in the afterlife, correct?"

He nodded. It was more than just an agreement with her words. His motion said so much more, as if what he'd learned about their boss, Cameron never wanted known by anyone.

"Maybe we can convince him that you did it for Holly's benefit. I mean, it's not like he gave us her full file." Which just spoke to how secretive Cameron wanted to be on their case.

Ian's hands relaxed on her arms. "You're right. We don't know when or how he will react."

She could tell he wasn't convinced in the least. He just wanted to pacify her. That he'd wanted to protect her had her heart singing, but that he did it at his own expense made her want to beat on his chest. "So can you at least tell me if you found anything in his file that says he really could make us disappear?"

Ian gave her a single nod, which sent a shiver down her spine. She lay down next to him again and his arm cradled her against him. "I won't let anything happen to you."

"And I won't let anything happen to you."

He squeezed her against him in response. In other words, she had no choice in what might happen. She absolutely refused to cry. It wasn't as if he was gone yet. There was still a chance for them.

Cold air brushed over her skin and she snapped her head up to find Cameron Douglas just inside the room. He was phased, but far larger than usual and his eyes sparked with anger.

Before she could let out a squeak, Ian had her flipped beneath him.

"HOW DARE YOU." Cameron's voice bounced off the walls of the room, vibrating the bed.

Ian's body above hers was as hard as stone. "It was necessary."

"Necessary?" She heard rather than saw Cameron turn solid and hit the floor with a thump. "What's necessary is the eradication of a spirit like yours that poisons those around it and has no respect for those above him. And there are so many above you Ian Fergusson."

"No!" She tried to wiggle out from beneath Ian's weight, but he wasn't moving.

"I must disagree with you. I learned information about your wife that you didn't know and it was necessary for me to determine the best course of action based upon your character."

"My character?" Cameron's voice boomed and Coco shuddered.

Shoot, Ian wasn't helping. Couldn't he see that?

"Yes, Cameron Douglas, you're character." Ian's chest expanded, clueing her in to his own anger. "The mysterious disappearance of Duncan Montgomerie and Jessica Thomas, the last two spirits you sent to your wife, your threats against myself and my partner and criticism on our efforts to help your wife, and the purposeful lack of information you supplied to enable us to be successful on our assignment, all equaled a need to determine your true character, so I could make a decision about whether I should share the additional information I've learned."

"If? If?" Her boss was clearly incredulous and probably about to lose it.

She understood that all too well when dealing with Ian. "Move." She pushed Ian with her palms, but he was solid rock. Scared for him, angry at her boss and frustrated, she gritted her teeth and tried one more time. When he didn't budge, she phased through him and solidified next to the bed to face her boss.

Cameron's eyes widened just before Ian wrapped her in her robe. Boy, the man moved fast.

Shoot. She'd faced her boss stark naked. Rattled, but determined, she pointed her finger at Cameron. "If you'd been honest with us from the beginning, we wouldn't have had to keep secrets from you or go around your back. Instead, you give us a file that was worthless and expect us to work miracles, which by the way we did."

"Coco." Ian's hands on her arms kept her from stepping as close to Cameron as she wanted.

"She's my wife." Cameron's look was hard and stubborn, so much like Ian that it didn't bother her one wit.

"Then you should do whatever is necessary to help her, not give us dribbles of information to work with. We shouldn't have to worry about how you'll react to what we discovered because your *wife* should come first."

"She does." Cameron's frown had not lessened but his tone of voice had.

She shook her head. "I don't think so." Even as she said it, the last piece of the puzzle slipped into place for her. Though she felt like jumping up and down in triumph, she settled for placing her hands on her hips.

"If that's the case then you have no problem with the fact that we discovered you have a half-sister and Holly plans to find her."

Cameron's mouth fell open.

She kept her smile to herself. "So you didn't know. Should Ian and I fear disappearing because you didn't know or didn't want to?"

Cameron shook his head, clearly confused. "How can that be?"

Ian pulled her against his side as if he could keep her from harm by being closer to Cameron. "My guess is your father had a relationship before he met your mother. We did not check to see if your aunt and uncle knew."

She studied her boss. Her goal was to save Ian. If she was right, getting rid of Ian had been Cameron's goal all along. She wasn't sure, but she had a feeling he'd hoped to get to Ian through her, but how was not clear…yet.

The silence became uncomfortable and as usual she just had to step in. "There is more, but I want a guarantee that Ian will not cease to exist."

"What?" Cameron's eyes widened.

"No." Ian pushed her behind him. "It is Coco who must remain here."

While she appreciated the thought, her gut told her she wasn't the one at risk. "Ian, stop, will you, or I'll just phase through you again."

He may have heard her, but he didn't move. Seriously? She peeked around his arm. Cameron glared at Ian. Ian had on his chiseled look in return.

"If you have something to tell me, I suggest you do so while you still can."

She tried to get in front of Ian, but he held her back. "Yes, I do. You should know that your wife has a soulmate. One who is still living."

Her boss immediately looked at her. "Is this true?"

She nodded.

"Who?"

She opened her mouth but Ian beat her to it. "Your best friend, Ethan."

She had expected Cameron to yell, maybe fly off the handle, or stare at them in rage, but none of that happened. Again, he looked at her and she nodded. "Soulmates are special. You can't mess with that."

That set him off, finally. "I know that! I've been a soulmate."

"*Been*, being the operative word." At Ian's harsh tone, she tugged on his arm, but he ignored her.

Cameron's eyes narrowed to slits. "It appears you have something you want to say to me."

Ian could feel Coco shake against him as her hands latched on for all she was worth. He loved her more than his existence, but that was ending soon and he had to keep her safe. It was time to bring the argument home to rest where it belonged. "You were so wrapped up in the next adrenaline rush, you couldn't appreciate what you had until it was too late. So now riddled with guilt, you use your position to try and make it right."

Cameron's body started to shake. "You know nothing about me. The file is nothing but actions." He thumped his chest with his fist. "I lived for Holly. I still exist for her. What do you exist for? You exist to punish yourself. Your own guilt makes you worthless to me."

Ian would have agreed with his supervisor before this case, but he understood better why he was a spirit guide, thanks to Coco. He also accepted that he was powerless to change Ella's fate. Plus, now he had something worth fighting for.

Using the steady tone he always had with his father, he didn't back down. "Even with my guilt, I improve the lives of the living. Yet with your guilt, you meddle in your wife's life. If she was your focus, why did you go mountain climbing on Christmas day? Why did you ignore Ethan's warning about the conditions? Did you have something to prove?"

Cameron's face turned red, but Ian continued. "I couldn't save Ella because she didn't want to be saved, but I can keep Coco safe. She is my world, and no one will hurt her. Can you say the same for Holly?"

"You bastard." Cameron's words were ground out between his teeth. He raised his arm.

Deep in his gut, Ian knew it was the end, but with all his being he didn't want it to be. "Like you, I found my soulmate."

Cameron froze.

The room continued in silence. He refused to look away from his superior, even when he felt Coco phase through him, sending warmth to every nook and cranny of his soul.

Her voice was soft as she solidified and spoke to Cameron. "It's true. Ian and I are soulmates."

Cameron's focus moved to her and Ian tensed, ready to throw her aside.

"Why didn't you tell me when I assigned you."

She shook her head. "I didn't know until later. All of a sudden we had matching glows, but I think we were always supposed to be. I just don't understand why I didn't know from the first time we met."

"Remiel." Cameron spoke the name softly.

"The arch angel?" Coco pushed her body back into Ian, and he wrapped his arms protectively around her.

Cameron nodded and his arm lowered. It appeared that Cameron did have limitations after all. At that realization, Ian felt the hope in his chest expand.

Coco held his arms about her waist. "Cameron, I once told Holly she couldn't change her past, only the future. I think what you're doing for her is admirable. It will change her future and I think yours as well…if you let it."

For the first time since he'd arrived, Cameron seemed to relax. "It appears despite everything that you two have succeeded with your assignment."

"Seriously?" Coco's shock mirrored Ian's own.

"Yes." Cameron sighed heavily, and there was far more to it than simply the conclusion of their work. For the first time, Ian felt a hint of sympathy for the man who he believed manipulated others even better than he could.

Cameron continued. "What Ian probably didn't share with you, is that the last two spirits who helped my wife did succeed. Despite what you heard, they voluntarily disappeared from our existence."

Coco gripped his arm tighter. "What do you mean?"

"I mean that after resolving their own issues, they were allowed to enter paradise."

Coco looked up at him. "You read that in the file?"

He nodded, a new peace starting to fill him. "Aye, I did."

She looked back at Cameron. "So you're saying we are spirit guides because we have to come to some kind of resolution with our lives?"

"That's exactly it. You always were sharp. Sharper than many others." Cameron looked pointedly at Ian.

He didn't take the bait, well aware that he had already moved farther along than his supervisor. He felt it mentally, physically and emotionally. He spoke to Coco instead. "I've come to understand that I could not have saved Ella as you told me from the start. If only I had listened to you."

Coco turned her back on Cameron and wrapped her arms around his neck. Her trust in him, made his heart swell.

"And I found my soulmate who was on his way to meet me anyway. We were just a little delayed."

He stared into the amber eyes of the woman he loved. The woman he was meant to be with for eternity. "But we are together now and will be forever. Are you ready for that?"

A low white glow surrounded them, becoming thicker to the point that he could no longer see their supervisor. All he could see was the woman in his arms, who smiled at him with pure joy. "Oh, I'm more than ready. How about you? Are you ready for a little hot Coco?" She wiggled her brows.

Ian laughed. "I think I'm going to want a lot more than that." He lifted her up so he could kiss her as they crossed into another realm all together.

"Oh, Ian."

Epilogue

Cameron sighed as he dropped into the easy chair in the corner of the room. That had been too close for comfort. With his first couple, he'd been surprised by almost losing Jessica, but with these two he'd almost mistakenly obliterated a spirit guide.

He'd let his own dislike of Ian almost get in the way of what was right. If that had happened, he would have failed. And worse, his interactions with Holly would have ended and his own existence would have been compromised.

The tasks he was given with these spirit guides in order to help his wife were becoming trickier and riskier, but he would do whatever it took to make Holly happy again.

He grinned and clasped his hands before him even as he stretched out his legs, crossing them at the ankles. So, Ethan was Holly's soulmate.

He'd hoped, but to have it confirmed gave him the will to keep going. Whatever task he was assigned next, he would accept it. He now knew he would have to be very careful how he handled it, which meant he was better prepared.

But first, he needed to say goodbye to his wife. It was his bonus for a job well done. Quickly, he stood and phased.

In an instant, he was dropping into his old living room. He smelled her sweet apple-cinnamon scent before he saw her. As he floated from the fireplace toward the tree, his gut reacted. She sat in his old chair in a bright green spaghetti-strap night gown that accentuated her breasts. It fell to mid-thigh where a red and white ruffle touched her skin.

He was more than a little jealous of that ruffle. Yet it warmed his heart to know she'd worn it for him. She must have dosed off waiting for him. Her lips were slightly parted as she breathed deeply in her repose, her dark lashes relaxed against her cheeks.

Mac jumped off Holly's chair and came over to rub against his legs. He still didn't understand how the cat could feel him in his phased state, but he bent over and gave it a good pat. In a way, he looked at Mac as Holly's guardian angel.

He floated closer. "Holly, love. Will you wake for me?"

"Cam?" Her confused voice as her eyelids fluttered open, tugged on his heart.

"Yes, it's me. Did you have fun at Brody's party?"

She smiled shyly. "It was good to see Brody and Sarah and Ethan and Mrs. Bell and, well everyone I guess. But it was hard without you holding my hand."

"Ah hen, I was with you in spirit."

She snorted. "Very funny."

He grinned. "I thought so."

"Oh, do you like my Christmas outfit?" She jumped up and twirled around which gave him a lovely view of the rounded bottom of her ass.

"It's beautiful. You grow prettier every day."

She laughed.

"Ach, it's good to hear you laugh." His soul energized at the sound, making the stress of his last encounter melt away.

Holly stopped moving. "I laughed a little at Brody's party. Were you there?"

He shook his head. "No, I had to finish up with Ian and Coco."

His wife smiled, filling his heart with love. "I really liked those two. You send me the best spirits."

He floated closer to her, wanting more than anything to take her in his arms. The need was so strong, he thought about phasing her, just for a minute.

"Cam, I miss you so much. Couldn't you visit me more often? Maybe once a week? Once a month if that's too much."

His gut twisted. "Hen, I shouldn't even be here now. I'm not even sure how much longer I'll be able to visit you."

As her eyes watered, he forgot to breathe.

"I miss you so much. This isn't how it was supposed to be." Tears started down her cheeks. "Coco said you were my soulmate. Soulmates love forever."

"Please don't cry, love. You tear out my heart with every tear." He lifted his hand to brush them from her cheek, but he couldn't feel her. The ache in his own chest grew unbearable and he spun away, furious that he'd done this to them, to her.

"No, don't leave. I'll stop." Holly's panicked voice froze him in place.

He didn't face her as he tried to regain his composure and his distance. He'd worked too hard for them to risk becoming trapped among the living. "We will love forever, I promise you." He finally turned to face her. "But we have to fully experience our time separate until we're together again."

She looked down and her lower lip came out just a bit. He would always nibble at it when he was alive—with her.

"Holly, look at me."

She lifted her gaze to him, the sorrow in her eyes like a knife to his gut. Despite that he forced a smile. "You have to live, don't you see? I need you to have a full life. It's the only thing that will give me peace. Please love, try for me?"

She pursed her lips and nodded.

"That's my girl." He floated closer. "I want you to be happy. I think I can call in a favor so I can see you again next Christmas, but a lot will depend on you."

"On me?" She crossed her arms. "How?"

"If I can make a case that you have been living a full life and are not simply waiting for me to visit again, then my superiors will give permission. But if you are still going through the motions, they will think I'm keeping you from moving on."

"Oh, that makes sense I guess from the spirit side of things."

His stomach loosened. "Exactly. But you can't pretend because spirits know. You have to get out there and truly live, get involved, care about others."

She smiled. "Oh don't worry about that. Coco and Ian left me with a whole list of people to see and help and I even promised to go to every Christmas party I'm invited to next year."

Relief seeped through him at her words. "That sounds like a great start. If you can do that for me, for us, I'll be allowed to visit again next Christmas." He floated close to her again. "I look forward to seeing you too, but I look forward to seeing you happy."

Holly reached her hand out and brought it through his body. The sensation filled the hollow places in his soul. "I promise. Knowing that you will be my reward, I can do that."

"I knew there was a reason I loved you." He gazed into her eyes a moment, her beautiful soul crystal clear to him. "Now I have to leave, but keep your promise and I will return."

She nodded. "Okay. Will you phase through me again? Please."

He grinned, this time feeling it to his toes. "It will be my pleasure."

She winked at him. "Mine too."

He laughed. "You're a handful, love. Now close your eyes."

As soon as she did, he floated through her, the satisfying sensation staying with him even as he flew through the ceiling, taking a piece of her essence with him.

This time he hung outside the roof and watched the Christmas lights in the street reflect off the new dusting of snow. The peace of the night coupled with the feeling of his wife gave him the determination he needed to move forward with the next step.

At the sound of the church bells chiming midnight, he flew into the ether, anxious to get started on plans for next Christmas.

For updates, sneak peeks, and special prizes, sign up to receive the latest news from Lexi at
https://app.mailerlite.com/webforms/landing/c1w1g3

Read on for an excerpt from *When Love Chimes*.

CHAPTER ONE

"I'm pregnant." Lynzie Mullins stared at the word "yes" on the home pregnancy test strip. Joy, fear, and anger collided inside her.

"Are you sure?" Her best friend, Coco Baker, grabbed the stick out of her hand. "Oh boy, that makes it pretty clear, but I've heard that you should get a real test done by a doctor. These aren't always accurate."

Lynzie nodded, still stunned. How could this have happened? Sure she wanted children someday, but she'd like to have a husband first. Cocktail waitressing wasn't that lucrative a profession and the only horse farm in town was falling apart, so training horses was out.

"You aren't going to tell him, are you?" Coco's question pulled her back to the issue at hand.

"Who?"

Coco rolled her eyes. "Andrew, who else? Unless you've been sleeping with someone other than him. I thought you guys use protection."

"We do." But she'd stopped taking the pill because of the expense. Besides Andrew could afford the really good condoms. She flopped down on the couch. Would Andrew help with child support? Would he insist on a DNA test? How much would that cost? Maybe he'd ask her to marry him.

Who was she kidding? He was nice and he loved having sex with her, but she knew he considered himself above her. He came from the new section of Lucasville.

They had fun together. It wasn't as if they were in love and while she hadn't slept with anyone while with him, she was pretty sure he had a few other women he slept with on a regular basis. Probably a perk of having money.

Coco sat down next to her. "What are you going to do?" Her friend's eyes were honestly concerned. Coco had too good of a heart. She also had a weird ability to recognize two people who were soulmates, but she never volunteered that information.

Maybe she should ask Coco if she and Andrew were soulmates. Then her worries would be over. "I don't know. I just found out. I'm still reeling a bit."

"A bit? If it was me, I think I'd faint." Coco laid back over the arm of the couch with the back of her hand on her forehead.

Lynzie smiled. She appreciated her friend trying to cheer her up. "I think I'll do what you said, go to a doctor. In the meantime, let's keep this between us."

Coco sat up and nodded. "Of course."

They sat in silence a few minutes before Coco crossed and re-crossed her legs. She really didn't like silence very much, especially when around others. "Not to change the subject, but I'm guessing you won't mind too much if I do. Did you hear that Ryan Crawford came back to town last night."

Lynzie's heart sped up at the very mention of her old high school crush. "No, I didn't hear."

Coco nodded. "Yup. According to Antony, he's come back to help his grandad sell his old horse farm. I haven't seen him yet, but I guess he looks a lot different."

Just great. "Why? Does he have limp, burn scars, a big tummy."

Coco laughed. "From what I hear, he's looking mighty good.

You don't have to work until later. Want to take a walk and see if we bump into him?"

She must be an idiot because she actually was contemplating Coco's idea. "No. I'm sure I'll run into him eventually."

Coco shrugged. "Suit yourself."

If she was going to suit herself, she would have run away with Ryan when he first left town. At this point in her life, she wasn't sure if she could handle meeting his wife and kids. "Maybe I should—"

A knock at her door interrupted her. She stood to answer it and Coco put her finger to her lips. If it was Andrew, she'd keep the baby stuff to herself. Actually, she'd keep it to herself until she'd had a doctor's visit.

She opened the door.

A man with dark hair and a white cowboy hat stood there filling out his t-shirt to its max. Her entire body took notice. Then he smiled, his white teeth gleaming against his tan skin. "Hi Lynzie."

He knew her? A customer at the bar maybe? She would have never missed such a hot hunk of a man. "I'm sorry, do I know you."

"Yeah, it's me. Ryan Crawford."

Read on for an excerpt of *Pleasures of Christmas Past.*

Chapter One

Jessica Thomas floated near the ceiling of the small Christmas ornament shop, anxiously waiting to find out who would be her mentor on this, her first case as a Spirit Guide. She had no idea what it would entail, which irritated her a little. When she was alive, she'd been an excellent social worker because she read the case file *before* meeting the client. The Spirit Guide position was very difficult to obtain, but her past expertise had helped her land the job and she was anxious to prove she deserved it.

Having the file would certainly help that.

She scanned the shop, liking the feel of the place. It was cozy, with ornaments everywhere in every conceivable shape and size. With just three days until Christmas the store was full of people, all with lovely Scottish accents. She'd never been to Scotland while alive, though she'd planned a trip once, but had to cancel. She'd just been too busy to take a vacation for any length of time. Yes, it was one of her many regrets she had about her short life. At least *she* felt thirty-three years was short.

As far as time went, her mentor was late, or at least it seemed like it. There was no time in the afterlife, a fact that had thrown her completely off balance, but she was learning to cope…somewhat. Maybe her mentor was still in class answering questions. One of the many instructors from the intensive training she'd gone through would be her mentor on this first assignment. She really liked old Archibald. He was an American from the 1880s. Mrs. Ferrisletter, from 1662 London, was very sweet and would be a lovely mentor. Jessica crossed her fingers. As long as she didn't get Dr. Marley, she'd be happy. That man could put a saint into a depression.

"Are you ready for your first case?" The lilt of a heavy Scottish accent behind her caused her to turn.

Duncan Montgomerie floated there, not close enough to touch, but near enough she caught the whiff of pine that was so much a part of him.

Oh no, not *him*. The man was the hottest instructor she'd had and even now she couldn't remember a word he'd said. She'd been too busy having her libido stroked by his voice while her eyes feasted on his rugged looks and ripped body. He'd never told them what time period he was from, but his accent gave him away as Scottish and some of his vocabulary made her think it might be centuries back, even though he dressed in modern-day clothes.

Nervousness tamped down her excitement. There was no way she'd be able to concentrate on this assignment with him around. She was bound to screw something up.

"Jessica?" His blue eyes sparkled with an unearthly light as one brow rose. "Are you with me, lass?"

"Yes, of course." She tried not to focus on his wavy brown hair that fell past his strong jawline or on his scruffy chin that led the eye to his quirking lips.

His arm stretched out past her as he pointed below them, revealing his forearm muscle flexing as he moved his finger. "That's our case. Mrs. Cameron Douglas."

Despite the butterflies tickling her stomach as Duncan's breath passed by her left ear, Jessica snapped her focus to the people below. There were many women in the shop. Mrs. Douglas could be any of them. She leaned away and looked her mentor in the eyes. "What's her first name?"

"Huh?"

Jessica pushed her glasses back up the bridge of her nose. "What's Mrs. Douglas' first name? To get a client to trust you, you must show an interest in them and knowing the person's first name is the very tip of the iceberg."

Duncan frowned. "I dinna teach you that."

She took a deep breath. "No, you didn't. It's part of the experience I bring to the job. Do you know her first name?"

He shook his head, clearly perplexed by her request.

"How long have you been a Spirit Guide?" It was really none of her business, but she wanted to be sure her mentor was, in fact, more experienced than she was.

He shrugged broad shoulders, drawing her focus back to his build.

"Since we have no time in the afterlife, I cannot tell you how long I've done this, but I can assure you it is no' my first case." He pulled the neck of his t-shirt away from his skin, as if it were too tight.

As far as she was concerned, the entire shirt was too tight with the way it molded to his chest muscles, showing a significant valley down the middle. Heck, if he just wanted to take the whole thing off, she certainly wouldn't complain.

"Holly." Duncan grinned and her insides turned to melting ice cream.

So why did he point out holly? It was Christmas. There was holly everywhere… And mistletoe. Oh, maybe she could find some mistletoe and Mr. Distraction here could catch the hint and kiss her.

"Holly is her first name." Duncan nodded to confirm his statement. "It's also what that older woman down there just called her."

Her? Oh right, the case. Jessica forced her gaze from Duncan and looked below. "Which one is she?"

"She's the owner of the shop. The one with the shoulder-length brown hair and red Christmas hat on."

Jessica forced herself to focus on the woman. Her straight hair was a very deep brown, like dark chocolate, and she had a round face with an adorable smile, but it didn't quite reach her eyes. There was a quiet sorrow about the friendly shop owner. She looked perhaps thirty years old, max. What could have caused such a poignant hurt in one so young? "She definitely has the Christmas spirit. Why does she need us?"

Duncan chuckled, a warm sound that sent pleasure from her heart to her fingertips and everywhere in between. "No' every case is about some old Scrooge character. Each person we're assigned needs something different, but it has to be very important for them. Cameron—he'll be our supervisor on this assignment—received special permission for us to tackle this. You can equate him to Marley in your Scrooge story. There is always a Sprit Guide supervisor who preps the person receiving our help."

"Cameron?" She couldn't resist looking at him again and was surprised to see him frown, an unusual occurrence for him.

"Cameron Douglas is—excuse me—*was* her husband. There is a strict rule about handling personal cases, but I guess Cameron made a good argument with the boss."

Even frowning, Duncan was gorgeous. His cheekbones were strong, but his nose did have a slight bump that kept him from being entirely perfect. Genetics? Or was that from an injury? She could see him modeling for a highland wool sweater catalog, looking scrumptious in a white turtleneck and tartan kilt. Oh. Just the idea of seeing this man in a kilt had her body flushing. What did they say about what a man wore under—

"Jessica? Are you listening?"

"What?" Oh no. She was afraid of this. "Sorry, my mind drifted. What were you saying?"

He studied her for a moment before explaining. "I said, we, or rather you officially, are one of three ghosts who will visit Mrs. Douglas. Our goal is to remind her of the happy times before she lost her husband. Cameron's wife is no' truly living, just going through the motions."

Jessica's heart melted for the woman. She'd had cases like this, but never tackled them with the ability she had now. The possibilities excited her, causing her adrenaline to kick in. "So we literally take her to wonderful moments in her past. This is going to be fun. I can already imagine her smiling and laughing." She couldn't help her own grin at the thought of bringing a client such joy.

Duncan raised his hand. "Hold on, it's no' that simple. Remember what I said in training?"

"Uh, you said a lot. What part?" Not that she remembered any of it.

"You cannot get too attached. You need to keep some distance. We only have one night to work our magic, so to speak." He grinned.

"Do you really believe that?" How could he be a trainer of Spirit Guides if he thought they could do any good staying detached?

His grin faded. "I wouldn't teach it if I dinna believe it. Trust me, lass, you cannot get too involved in someone else's troubles. If you do, your soul will become entangled with your case."

She stared, open-mouthed. Had she really missed how shallow he was in the training? Or maybe he was talking from experience. She studied him closer. Was there something substantial behind those good looks?

His grin returned. "But dinna worry. I'll be there to help." His comment was said with such arrogance that for the first time she found herself not liking him at all.

She wasn't exactly a novice at this. It may be her first case as a

Spirit Guide, but she did have years of experience as a social worker. Maybe she needed to focus on the client and not on Mr. Distraction. "Where's the file?"

"Dinna worry about that. I can give you all the basics." Again he smiled, but this time, she noticed it was the kind a person gives to a child when humoring them.

He had little faith she could accomplish this assignment. Well, he was in for a surprise. She had a mission of her own and that was to prove Duncan Montgomerie was no more than a redundancy on this mission. Pasting on a fake smile, she took charge of *her* case. "I appreciate that, but I'd like to read through the file anyway. Sometimes, as a woman, I can catch a clue or two when trying to better understand a female client."

He shrugged once again and she forced herself to focus on his face.

"I left it on your desk. When you're done looking for *clues*, let me know and we can get started." He was clearly laughing at her.

She gritted her teeth. This wouldn't work. She would have to request another mentor because it was obvious the two of them had radically different ideas about helping people. She forced her jaw to loosen. "Fine." Without another word, she floated through the ceiling and back to her office to plan her attack and have a talk with her new supervisor.

Duncan watched Jessica drift away and chuckled. The lass was "wound too tight," as he'd heard Cameron say. Even her look was too professional. Blonde hair pulled back into a loose ponytail, wire-rimmed glasses hiding very bonny green eyes and a buttoned-to-the-neck Oxford shirt that made her look more like a scholar than a counselor. Her navy-blue pantsuit was boxy, hiding her entire body, and reminded him of a Christmas candle, rectangle bottom with a bright round flame at the top.

There was no way she would get through her first case without messing up. Good thing he was her mentor. He couldn't see any of the other instructors dealing well with her. He dinna doubt her heart was in the right place, but helping the living while dead was very different from helping them while alive.

He had a hard time remembering what it was like no' having the ability to move through space and time at will. It had been so long since he died. He frowned. It was difficult remembering the exact year, but he was confident it was long ago. He'd trained too many recruits. No' that it mattered. Time meant nothing now.

He grinned. Training new Spirit Guides was a fun adventure and he was perfectly happy where he was. It would be entertaining to watch the lass handle her first assignment. And when she stumbled, because she definitely would, he'd be there to catch her. The idea of what she might feel like under all those clothes had his smile widening. First, she needed to lose the glasses and the ponytail. Then he'd be happy to help her change into something more comfortable. Something he would do as soon as this assignment was over. The clothing in his time period was much less confining, but dressing according to the year of the client helped keep the person from running away in pure horror when he showed up.

Activity below caught his attention and his smile faded. He watched their client as Holly helped a teenager choose a unique ornament for his girlfriend.

Cameron and his wife had had one of those rare love stories that deserved a happily forever after, no' just a happily for thirteen months. Duncan had no idea what that was like, but he respected it. To see two people so in love suddenly separated by death touched even his hardened bachelor's soul.

Though he'd only known Cameron for a short while, probably almost a year, it was clear the man was a brilliant supervisor, but like his wife, sadness emanated from his spirit. Holly deserved a wee bit of happiness herself and Cameron could benefit from a little peace. If Duncan could do this small service for him, he would.

And there was no blasted way he would let Miss Jessica Thomas bumble their assignment, bonny eyes or no'.

Also by Lexi Post

Paranormal Romance

Masque

Passion's Poison

Passion of Sleepy Hollow

Pleasures of Christmas Past (A Christmas Carol Series: Book 1)

Desires of Christmas Present (A Christmas Carol Series: Book 2)

Temptations of Christmas Future (A Christmas Carol Series: Book 3)
Coming 2017

Sci-fi Romance

Cruise into Eden (The Eden Series: Book 1)

Unexpected Eden (The Eden Series: Book 2)

Eden Discovered (The Eden Series: Book 3)

Eden Revealed (The Eden Series: Book 4) Coming 2017

Contemporary Cowboy Romance

Cowboys Never Fold (Poker Flat Series: Book 1)

Cowboy's Match (Poker Flat Series: Book 2)

Cowboy's Best Shot (Poker Flat Series: Book 3)

Cowboy's Break (Poker Flat 4)

Christmas with Angel (Last Chance Series: Book 1)
Trace's Trouble (Last Chance Series: Book 2)
Fletcher's Flame (Last Chance: Book 3)
Logan's Luck: (Last Chance Series: Book 4)
When Love Chimes
Coming December 2016

About Lexi Post

Lexi Post is a New York Times and USA Today best-selling author of romance inspired by the classics. She spent years in higher education taking and teaching courses about the classical literature she loved. From Edgar Allan Poe's short story "The Masque of the Red Death" to Tolstoy's *War and Peace*, she's read, studied, and taught wonderful classics.

But Lexi's first love is romance novels. In an effort to marry her two first loves, she started writing romance inspired by the classics and found she loved it. From hot paranormals to sizzling cowboys to hunks from out of this world, Lexi provides a sensuous experience with a "whole lotta story."

Lexi is living her own happily ever after with her husband and her cat in Florida. She makes her own ice cream every weekend, loves bright colors, and you will never see her without a hat.

www.lexipostbooks.com